# Secrets in the Sand

Sharon Siamon

# Secrets in the Sand

**Original title:** Secrets in the Sand
**Cover and inside illustrations:** © 2006 Jennifer Bell
**Cover layout:** Stabenfeldt A/S
Typeset by Roberta L. Melzl
Editor: Bobbie Chase
Printed in Germany, 2007

ISBN: 1-933343-51-6


Stabenfeldt, Inc.
457 North Main Street
Danbury, CT 06811

www.pony.us

# Contents

# Chapter 1
# Vet's Verdict

Kelsie MacKay stood with the toes of her barn boots in the ocean. "An – dy! Jen!" she shouted. "Caspar's getting worse … the roof's leaking like crazy. Come and help!"

"In a minute!" her brother bellowed from his boat, which was coming into Dark Cove. Her friend Jen waved from the bow.

Kelsie watched them chug slowly toward her Aunt Maggie's dock. Seagulls circled over the motorboat, screaming. The sea looked dark and angry and a north wind blew gusts of rain in Kelsie's face. No use waiting for them. Andy took forever to tie up his precious boat. You'd think he was docking a cruise ship, the way he fussed over that green dory. And why was Jen out there with him?

Hurrying back to the leaky barn and her horse, Caspar, Kelsie had a flash of galloping the white horse along this same shore on a bright summer day. His hooves had kicked up the surf – his wet coat had thrown off drops of water like diamonds in the sun. Now the big horse slumped in his stall, eyes half shut, barely moving.

It was her fault. Caspar got sick after a moonlight swim to Saddle Island through icy ocean water. That swim had been her idea. Since then it had rained solidly for two weeks, as though Nova Scotia's Eastern Shore had forgotten it was summer.

Kelsie crossed the wet grass of her Aunt Maggie's yard and yanked open the barn door.

There was a new drip – right on Caspar's head. He twitched every time a drop hit him. Kelsie put him in another stall and dried him as well as she could with an old saddle blanket. She knew Caspar needed a vet but her Aunt Maggie had no money, not one spare cent, to pay vet bills.

Drip, drip, drip. The buckets were overflowing.

What was taking Andy and Jen so long?

Kelsie closed Caspar's stall door. She stomped up and down the barn, dumping pails into a large rain barrel. Her jeans were soaked, her rubber boots squelched with every step, her auburn hair was twisted into knots it would take hours to brush out, and her face was streaked with stall dirt. Kelsie didn't care. Nothing mattered but Caspar.

Buckets empty, Kelsie went over to rest her cheek on Caspar's snowy white one. "We'll get you better," she whispered. "Jen will be here to help in a minute – and she loves you almost as much as I do." Her friend Jen had helped hatch the plot that saved Caspar from the auction block two weeks before. She knew a lot about horses.

But when the door creaked open behind Kelsie a few minutes later it wasn't Jen. To her astonishment Kelsie saw the vet, Dr. Bricknell, and her Aunt Maggie step into the leaky old barn, dodging drips.

Dr. Bricknell had deep grooves in his narrow face and thin white hair. He strode over to Caspar's stall and opened his black case. "I presume this is Caspar?" he said gruffly. "Your aunt said I should come right away."

"Thank you, Aunt Maggie," Kelsie gulped. Her aunt must have hated to call Dr. Bricknell, but she'd done it anyway.

Maggie Ridout nodded, her lips pressed together.

Kelsie wanted to throw her arms around her aunt, but there was something about the stern, middle-aged woman that said, "hands off." She was tall and lean, with iron gray hair pulled back from her high forehead with two silver clips. Her yellow rain slicker was hugged tight over her chest.

Kelsie turned back to Caspar and Dr. Bricknell. His face was even more creased than usual as he held a stethoscope to the big horse's chest.

Just then, the barn door creaked again. Kelsie glanced up quickly. Jen, at last!

Jen threw back the hood of her raincoat. "How is Caspar?" she asked.

Kelsie shook her head. "Worse today. I'm *so* glad Aunt Maggie called Dr. Bricknell."

As the vet listened, the white horse stood patiently. The only sounds were his harsh breathing, the patter of rain on the metal roof and the drip, drip of water from a leak in the roof into a bucket.

Drip, drip, like the beat of a heart. Kelsie felt her own thump as she waited for Dr. Bricknell's verdict on Caspar's condition. "Don't say he's going to die," she begged silently. "Don't tell us it's hopeless."

She knew Caspar had been too long in the icy water, worked too hard to bring her safe through the wind and waves to the shore of Saddle Island. And she'd taken him back in the freezing ocean to save his owner, Hank Harefield, when his boat ran aground in the storm.

Harefield had been so grateful he'd given Caspar to Kelsie, to live in Aunt Maggie's ancient barn.

Just then, Caspar groaned. Kelsie grabbed for Jen's hand. She felt Jen interlace her fingers through hers and squeeze hard. They were in this together.

Her Aunt Maggie stood apart from them. Kelsie didn't dare look at her. Aunt Maggie would be thinking of the drip, drip of money going down the drain as Dr. Bricknell poked and prodded and hemmed and hawed.

Finally, the vet stepped away from Caspar. He took the stethoscope out of his ears, folded it carefully and shoved it into his jacket pocket.

"His lungs are congested with the flu," he said, still looking at the horse. "But his heart is strong and his belly sounds are good. No sign of colic."

He took a pen and pad out of another pocket and wrote quickly. "Get this medication and give it to him twice a day." He handed the prescription to Aunt Maggie. "And try to get the roof fixed as soon as you can. This horse needs a dry stall with the summer so wet and cold."

Aunt Maggie nodded grimly. Kelsie knew there was probably no money for medicine and none to fix the roof, either.

The vet turned to Kelsie and Jen. "There's something else. Caspar needs more than medicine and a dry bed if you want him to recover completely. He needs company."

9

"Company?" Aunt Maggie spoke up. "I don't see how the horse could be wanting more company. Kelsie practically lives in this wreck of a barn."

Dr. Bricknell rubbed Caspar's face thoughtfully. "That's fine, but it isn't human company Caspar needs. I'm sure he misses the other school horses up at Harefield Farms." The vet paused. "I hear the stable's for sale."

"It's been sold." Jen nodded. "Some rich guy from Boston bought it, this week."

"That happened fast." Dr. Bricknell raised his eyebrows. "Do you know what will happen to the other horses?"

Jen and Kelsie glanced at each other. "N-no," stammered Jen.

"They might be for sale." Kelsie said eagerly. "If …"

"Don't even think about it." Aunt Maggie's mouth was a thin line. "No more horses."

"It wouldn't have to be a horse." The vet gave Caspar a final pat, stepped out and closed the stall door. "A goat or a dog makes a good stable mate for a horse."

"No more animals." Aunt Maggie held up her hand. "We can't look after the one we have."

"Not even a dog?" Kelsie asked hopefully. "Andy would love a dog."

"No dogs," Aunt Maggie said firmly. "And no goats either. Thank you, Dr. Bricknell, I'll walk you to your car."

"Call me if there's any change." Dr. Bricknell looked up at the dripping roof. "And get those leaks fixed."

◆◆◆◆◆

After the vet and Aunt Maggie had closed the barn door, Kelsie buried her face in Caspar's long white mane. "We've got to fix the roof and find you a stable mate." She looked up at Jen. "I wish we *could* buy one of Harefield's horses." Her voice rose in excitement. "Maybe Zeke – he was your favorite, wasn't he?"

Jen had worked at the riding stable, mucking out stalls and helping look after the school horses. "I *love* Zeke," she sighed. "But I'm not making any money, helping Mom at the restaurant. I wish I had a real job."

"Jobs!" Kelsie kicked clean straw around Caspar's feet. " I'm only thirteen and you're still twelve. We have to go to school. How could we get jobs? Even my dad can't find one."

"What do you mean?" Jen looked startled. "I thought your father had a great job in a diamond mine up north. Isn't that why you and Andy came to live with your Aunt Maggie in the first place?"

"The mine closed. Not the first time *that's* happened." Kelsie twisted her tangled hair between her fingers. "I hope we don't have to move again. I wish there was work here in Dark Cove for Dad."

Jen shrugged. "Not unless he has a lobster boat like Gabe Peters."

"Yeah, like Gabriel." At the mention of his name, a picture sprang into Kelsie's mind of seventeen year-old Gabe Peters standing on the deck of his father's fishing boat, looking tall and proud like the prince of Dark Cove. He was one of the main reasons she didn't want to leave.

Jen broke into her thoughts. "Listen, I have to go. I promised Mom I'd help her in the Clam Shack tonight."

"All right." Kelsie sighed, wishing Jen could stay longer. "I meant to ask you – why were you out in Andy's boat today?"

"I … um … he wanted me to go." Jen shrugged. "So I went." She opened the barn door and the wind whipped back her brown hair.

"That's not much of a reason. Please, just tell me what you see in my demented little brother?"

Jen didn't answer. She stood in the doorway, not moving, listening.

"What's wrong?" Kelsie stepped out of Caspar's stall.

"Somebody's calling … down at the dock." Jen flipped up her jacket hood. "It's Andy. Sounds like he needs help." She flew out the door, leaving it banging.

Kelsie quickly closed Caspar's stall door and tore after Jen, pausing long enough to shut the barn door.

Now she could hear her brother, too. He was shouting for help from the long dock that stuck out in front of Aunt Maggie's house.

## Chapter 2
# Save My Boat!

Kelsie and Jen ran down the wood dock. To their right, waves slapped against the big cement pier of the old fish plant. To their left, the ocean met a small sandy point. Past the point the surf boomed on a strip of beach that curved away to a huge rock called the Grinder. Lots of small boats and ships had been lost on the Grinder, beaten to pieces by the sea.

"My boat!" Andy was bellowing. "It's getting away. Help me."

Andy's green motorboat was skimming away over the water, drifting farther from the shore with every second.

Kelsie and Jen plunged down a steep wood ramp to a floating raft at the bottom. At high tide the float would be almost level with the main dock. Now, when the tide was at its lowest, the two girls had to grip lifelines on either side of the ramp to keep from catapulting into the water.

Andy was crouched on the float. It bucked and bobbed in the rough water like a running horse. He was hugging a heavy outboard motor that threatened to slide into the dark sea.

"What happened?" Kelsie cried. "Gabriel just fixed that motor for you. Why on earth did you take it off your boat?"

"One of the bolts that holds it broke." Andy's face was scarlet with the effort of holding onto the bulky motor. His short blond hair stuck up in wet spikes. "I thought the other one might go, too."

"Never mind that, now." Jen said, her eyes fixed on the drifting boat. "If she gets around the point, she'll smash up on the Grinder." Jen had lived in Dark Cove, on the eastern shore of Nova Scotia, all her life. She could read the ocean like the daily paper.

"What am I going to do?" Andy begged.

"I might be able to catch her in my kayak," said Jen.

"Good idea." Kelsie nodded. "I'll help you get her launched."

Leaving Andy hugging his precious motor on the float, the

two girls sprang up the ramp. Jen's red kayak, the *Seahorse*, was beached above the high tide line near the dock. Jen handed Kelsie the double-ended paddle while she carried the *Seahorse* over the seaweed and slippery rocks to the water. She plunged in without paying any attention to her wet feet and jeans, lowered herself into the cockpit and reached back for the paddle.

"It'll be a race to catch her before she rounds the point," Jen grunted, wiggling her feet into position.

"Don't take any chances," warned Kelsie. "It's just an old boat." She waded into the water to hand Jen her paddle. Even in August, the sea was cold.

"It's Andy's boat!" Jen grabbed the paddle. "It means as much to him as Caspar does to you."

Kelsie watched while Jen spurted forward, scooping the paddle into the water on either side. It would be a race, all right. The farther Andy's boat got from shore, the faster it drifted. The wind was blowing harder.

"Kelsie! Come back and help me," she heard Andy shout. "I'm slipping." A sudden lurch of the float had sent the motor sliding across its wet surface. Andy tried to slow it down, but any second he'd be in the water, too. Kelsie knew her brother would rather sink to the bottom than let his motor go.

She stumbled to shore over the slimy rocks, trying to reach him.

But someone else was already running down the dock – a man, a strange, tall man wearing a black all-weather jacket.

"It's all right. You can let go." The man seized the motor from Andy and lifted it with one hand. He passed Kelsie on his way up the ramp. "Where should I put this?"

"In the fish house." Kelsie pointed to a dilapidated shack at the top of the dock.

"Who is that?" Andy gasped, staring after the tall man.

"Don't know," Kelsie said breathlessly. "He just appeared out of nowhere. Look –" She turned Andy around and pointed to the sea where the kayak dipped and rose over the waves.

"GO, Jen!" Andy urged, his hands balled into fists. "I've

got to have my boat. How can I look for treasure on Saddle Island with no boat?"

"You're not going to find treasure on the island. Forget that stupid idea."

"But we need money –" Andy broke off. "Hey! Jen's almost got her."

Jen had caught up to the fleeing boat. She paddled past it, then spun the kayak around and came alongside to reach for its bow rope.

"She saved my boat." Andy's grin stretched from ear to ear. "She's so brilliant."

Kelsie gave him a sharp glance. She suspected her twelve-year-old brother admired more than Jen's paddling. She'd seen the way he looked at her – like an adoring puppy.

The float suddenly gave a lurch as the man in the black jacket jumped down beside them. "The motor's safe in the fish house," he said, smiling. "Does your brave buddy out there need any help?"

"She's okay." Kelsie was watching Jen closely. The drag of Andy's boat made the kayak swerve from side to side, but Jen was making headway with the wind behind her.

"Thanks for helping me." Andy glanced shyly up at the man.

"I'm glad I came along when I did." The man smiled. "My name's Paul Speers. Your aunt said I'd find you down by the water – I don't think she knew you were in trouble."

"And don't tell her," Andy said quickly. "Aunt Maggie worries enough about me and my dory. She might take it away if she knew."

"Fine with me." The man peered out at Andy's boat, zigzagging behind the kayak. "But she's not really a dory, is she? Too small. I'd call your boat a skiff, or maybe a tender."

Andy flushed. "Dad calls her a dory," he mumbled.

Kelsie was studying Paul Speers closely. If she was right, his jacket was expensive, and his hair, even though it was long, was well cut. He looked like one of the mine managers or geologists you saw fly into a northern mining town for a day or two. Rich, but casual. "Why were you looking for us?" she asked.

"You must be Kelsie." Paul Speers stuck out his hand. "I've just bought Harefield Farms. Your aunt says you have one of their horses."

"That's right." Kelsie frowned. She started up the ramp to help Jen beach the kayak and drag Andy's boat ashore.

He followed. "Hold on a minute. I have an offer for you I don't think you'll want to refuse."

Kelsie whirled to look at him. What offer?

Did he want Caspar back?

# Chapter 3
# Good Deal

"Hank Harefield gave Caspar to me," Kelsie told Paul Speers, "and he's not for sale, at any price."

She didn't dare meet Aunt Maggie's steel-gray eyes. She knew her aunt would leap at the chance to sell Caspar.

They were in the kitchen of her aunt's small blue house, having tea and blueberry scones. Andy and Paul Speers sat on one side of the table, Kelsie and Aunt Maggie on the other.

Jen had gone to the Clam Shack to help her mother. As she left, Kelsie had watched her give Andy a small wave over her shoulder. It was depressing, but Jen seemed to *like* her skinny little brother. Jen had never given her a special wave like that. It was almost like a secret signal between them.

Mr. Speers was good-looking, Kelsie decided, looking at him across the table, with his square shoulders, dark blue eyes, and a smile that showed off perfect teeth. He wore jeans and riding boots he'd politely taken off in the hall. That had impressed Aunt Maggie so much she'd invited him to tea.

"I don't want to buy Caspar," he said, putting down his mug. "I have big plans for Harefield Farms. I want to establish a stud farm on the property."

"Then I suppose you'll be tearing everything down and building a great big house overlooking the ocean." Aunt Maggie looked down her straight nose at Paul Speers.

"Nothing like that." He laughed. "I don't intend to change a thing. In fact I've been searching up and down the coast for a place just like it – a real heritage property."

Kelsie could see the lines on Aunt Maggie's forehead relax. "More tea?" she offered.

"Thank you." Paul Speers held out his mug.

"What's a stud farm?" Andy asked. His eyes hadn't left Speers' face since they sat down.

"I want to breed race horses," Paul Speers explained. "So

you can see I won't have room for the school horses that are living at the farm. But I'd like to find good homes for them, if I can. So …" He pointed a finger at Kelsie, "…when I heard you had one of Harefield's horses I thought, who better to take the rest?"

Kelsie gasped. "You want to just give the horses to us, Mr. Speers?"

"I'm afraid they'd be hard to sell." Speers rubbed his smooth jaw. "And I hate to see them go to the canning factory."

Aunt Maggie was shaking her head sadly. "We can't accept," she said. "We can't look after Caspar, let alone three more horses."

Kelsie was thinking how wonderful it would be. They'd have company for Caspar to help him get well. He'd be part of a small herd with Zeke and Midnight and Sailor, the Newfoundland pony. Maybe they were just school horses. Maybe they weren't worth much, but to her they were friends.

"I'm afraid it's impossible. Feed and hay for three horses and a pony, vet fees and farrier's bills – it would cost a fortune," Aunt Maggie was saying. "On top of that, my barn leaks."

"Oh, we could get your barn fixed." Paul Speers waved away her objection with a well-manicured hand. "I'm going to have a crew of workmen up at the farm. I could send them down to repair your roof."

"It's a very nice offer," Aunt Maggie sighed, "but there's no pasture here, and even if there was, I couldn't afford hay for the winter. When this was a farm, years ago, we had pasture and hay fields out on Saddle Island. That's all gone now –"

"No, it isn't!" Kelsie leaped to her feet, almost knocking over a chair. "Please, Aunt Maggie, think about it. There's still pasture in the middle of Saddle Island. We could keep the horses there for the rest of the summer and fall, and then –"

She stopped short, staring at her aunt, who scraped back her chair and stood up.

"And then – what? You and your wild dreams." She shook her head back and forth firmly. "I've told you. You can't take the horses and that's that. It's a ridiculous idea."

"Wait, just a second," Paul Speers said. He smiled at Aunt Maggie and motioned her to sit back down. "People used to tell me I was a dreamer, too. But I've made millions selling my 'ridiculous' ideas. One bit of software that I invented is in almost every computer in the world. That's why I can retire at thirty-five and devote my life to breeding race horses." He looked at Andy and Kelsie. "Tell me about this island of yours."

"I'll get the map." Kelsie dashed up the stairs before Aunt Maggie could protest. She was back in a flash with a yellowed old map in a wood frame. She plunked it down in the middle of the table, facing Paul Speers.

"This is Aunt Maggie's island." Kelsie pointed to faint dots on the map. "These dots used to be a farm," she went on. "With a house and a barn and a wishing spring."

"There were pirates and smugglers on Saddle Island too," Andy added. "There might be –" He changed the subject, suddenly not wanting Mr. Speers to hear about buried treasure on the island. Something about this man bothered him. He was sure his dad wouldn't like him. "How do you know my boat's not a dory?" he asked instead.

"Boats are my hobby, along with horses." Speers smiled his wide smile. "I love everything to do with the ocean."

"Is he right?" Andy interrupted, looking straight at his aunt. "Dad said it was a dory."

Aunt Maggie nodded. "Mr. Speers is correct. Your father liked to think he had an old-fashioned Nova Scotia dory, but he was wrong. Real dories are double-ended and heavier. Mr. Speers knows his boats."

Kelsie could hear in her aunt's voice that she was weakening. She broke in. "You said you wished Saddle Island could be a farm again, remember?"

Aunt Maggie put her strong hand on Kelsie's shoulder. "Yes, I did say that," she murmured. "But that was before your father lost his job, and my pension from the fish plant got cut back. We're not in a position to take on the expense of three more horses. You know that."

"I'm sure I could help with expenses," murmured Speers. "In the meantime, would it be all right if the kids took me

18

out to this famous island in Andy's boat?" He smiled at Aunt Maggie. "I'd love to see the place. I'm very interested in the history of this coast. "

"Tomorrow," Kelsie blurted out. "Could we go tomorrow? We'll show you the old farm."

◆◆◆◆◆

Later, when Speers had gone, and Aunt Maggie had driven off to buy Caspar's medicine, Kelsie checked on her horse.

Andy followed her to the barn.

Caspar was just as before. Head down, nose running. "I'm sure the medicine will help him," Kelsie said rubbing his forehead gently, "but if we had all his buddies on Saddle Island, he'd soon be his old goofy self, galloping along the shore."

Caspar bobbed his head, as if he agreed.

Andy leaned over the stall door. "But four horses cost a lot of money, Kel. What if Aunt Maggie can't feed them? What if she can't feed us? We might have to leave Dark Cove."

Kelsie turned on her brother, green eyes flashing. "Don't be crazy. You heard Paul Speers, didn't you? He's going to help us keep the horses on the island. If we can just get Aunt Maggie to agree, everything will work out. Anyway, Aunt Maggie would never send us away. She cares about us – look how she called the vet when Caspar needed him."

"I hope you're right." Andy sighed. "I don't want to move away. Not now that I've got my boat running so well, and Gabriel and I are friends."

"And Jen?" Kelsie shot Andy a look. "I suppose you think she's your friend now. What was she doing out there with you in the boat today – in the rain?"

"Nothing. Just messin' around. None of your business." Andy blushed and changed the subject. "Tomorrow I'm going to search that smuggler's hideout you and Jen found on Saddle Island."

Kelsie rolled her eyes at him. "I told you before – you're not going to find anything except cobwebs in that old hole."

"You always think you know everything," Andy muttered. "We'll see, tomorrow." He went out, banging the barn door behind him.

Kelsie straightened Caspar's forelock where it fell in his eyes. "You hang in," she told the big white horse. "I'm sleeping right here in the barn with you tonight."

◆◆◆◆◆

Early in the morning the rain stopped.

Kelsie woke up to the sounds of Caspar munching hay and Jen gently sweeping the barn floor. She shot out of her sleeping bag and peered over the stall division.

"How is he?" Sunshine was streaming through the small barn window onto Caspar's white hide. He picked up his head and gave a soft whinny as she reached over to stroke his neck.

"Better, I think," said Jen. "You …" She laughed. "You look like you slept in a stall."

"I did. I wanted to be close – in case." Kelsie pulled strands of straw out of her auburn curls. "What's the weather like? Will we be able to get to the island today?"

"Calm as a flat blue plate out there." Jen grinned. "Andy's already got the motor bolted back on the boat – we're just waiting for the wonderful Paul Speers."

"Don't you like him?" Kelsie couldn't miss the sarcasm in Jen's voice.

Jen kept her head down, sweeping. "Well, Mom sure does. Speers turned up at the Clam Shack for breakfast and she acted as jumpy as the bacon on the griddle."

Kelsie knew Jen's mother, Chrissy, had been alone since Jen was a baby. She could see how a guy like Paul Speers would make a big impression on her. "What's wrong with that?" she asked.

"I don't know. Something about Speers is too slick." Jen shook her head. "Why does he want to be so helpful?"

"Why are *you* so suspicious!" Kelsie exclaimed. "Maybe Paul Speers just wants to make friends in a new place. It's not easy. I've lived in five mining towns since I was born, and every place I had to prove myself all over again." She smiled at Jen. "Except here, in Dark Cove. Here I was family, right from the start. Dad's family has been here for six generations."

Jen's soft blue eyes were sympathetic. "All right. I'll try to like Mr. Fancy Stud Farm –" she stopped with a laugh. "I guess I'd better not call him *that*."

Just then, Andy burst into the barn.

"Come on!" he shouted. "Mr. Speers is here. He's brought a cooler full of food from the Clam Shack. I hope it doesn't swamp the dory – I mean the skiff."

"Whoa." Kelsie pulled back her hair and brushed the straw off her jeans. "I have to get changed and cleaned up. Give me ten minutes and we can shove off for Saddle Island."

"We'll wait for you down at the dock," Jen called over her shoulder. She seemed in an awful hurry to go running off with Andy, Kelsie noticed.

# Chapter 4
# Island Secret

Andy's green skiff chugged into the narrow passage between Saddle Island and Teapot Island to the west. Today, the gulls soared over the sunlit water, at peace with the wind and the world.

Kelsie pointed to a row of large rocks lurking just under the surface of the narrow passage like a row of pointed black teeth. "Those rocks used to be a road, like a causeway, linking the islands to the mainland," she shouted to Paul Speers over the outboard's roar.

"What happened to the causeway?" he shouted back.

"It washed away in a big storm. But the rocks will still rip the bottom out of your boat unless you come in at high tide," Kelsie told him. She couldn't wait to explore Saddle Island again. It was the third island out from Maggie Ridout's dock – shaped like a saddle – high at both ends and low in the middle. Beyond it, the Atlantic Ocean stretched all the way to Africa.

If only Aunt Maggie would agree to let them bring the horses here.

Beside her, Aunt Maggie's face was stern, with strands of gray hair blowing across her forehead. For her, Kelsie thought, this island was a place of good and terrible memories. Until the big storm two weeks ago, the night Caspar got sick, she hadn't visited it for twenty-five years.

On Aunt Maggie's other side, Jen sat squished under the cooler of food Speers had bought at the Clam Shack. Saddle Island was special to her, too. Before Kelsie and Andy had arrived, she had been the island's only visitor for years, kayaking out from Dark Cove, and climbing the cliff called the Saddle Horn at the island's northern end.

Andy steered the skiff into a natural harbor, a groove in the island's rocky shore. He tied her to a tree while the others unloaded the skiff on the smooth gray rocks.

"C'mon, Jen. This way, Mr. Speers, Aunt Maggie." Kelsie pointed down a narrow path through a tangle of blackberry vines. She danced with impatience. "Andy, bring that cooler."

"You take it." Andy scrambled up from the mooring. "I'm going for a walk."

Kelsie turned, frowning. "Andy, we're here to show Mr. Speers the old farm and the pasture – to see if the Harefield Farms horses can live on the island. Remember?"

"You go," Andy said stubbornly. "I want to look for something."

"That old smuggler's stash?" Kelsie frowned, her hands on her hips. "For Pete's sake, Andy, you're not going to find anything in there."

"What's he looking for?" Speers came up between them.

"Nothing." Andy scrunched up his eyes. He didn't want Speers butting in. "I won't be long," he promised Kelsie.

"You'll never find it on your own."

"I'll go with Andy," Jen muttered to Kelsie. "He's not going to give up till he sees what's down in that dirty old hole. You go ahead with Mr. Speers and your aunt."

"Oh, all right." Kelsie sounded exasperated. "If Aunt Maggie says it's okay – Andy's all yours. He's so totally fixated on finding old rum-smuggling money. As if –"

Aunt Maggie gave her permission. "I know you'll keep him out of trouble," she told Jen, with a smile. She, Kelsie and Paul Speers started down the overgrown path while Jen and Andy headed in the opposite direction.

◆◆◆◆◆

Jen led the way, a long length of rope coiled over her shoulder. She tried to remember the route she and Kelsie had taken two weeks before – through the trees, across rocks, shallow bogs and meadow grass. The island was long – it would take all day to walk from one end to the other – but the smuggler's hideout was almost straight across from the landing place near the farm.

"Here. It should be here." Jen fell to her knees in a patch of long grass. "Look out, Andy." She pulled back the grass to uncover a square hole in the dirt, almost overgrown. It was an old smugglers' hideout, called a stash.

"Wow!" Andy breathed. "No wonder Harefield fell in. He couldn't see the hole."

"Caspar knew it was here." Jen grinned. "He wouldn't take another step when we got to this place." She knotted the rope around a large rock. The other end she dropped into the hole. "Lower yourself slowly," she warned Andy. "It's a long way down."

Andy shoved his flashlight in his jeans' pocket, gripped the rope with both hands and slid into the hole. Soon all Jen could see was the top of his spiky hair.

"I'm at the bottom," he said a few seconds later as the rope went slack. His voice sounded hollow.

"What do you see?" Jen called.

There was a long pause.

"Andy? Are you all right?"

"Come down here," Jen heard him shout. "It's cool!"

Jen made sure the rope was not going to slip off the rock. If it did they'd be stuck in the hole for a long time, like Mr. Harefield. He had been sound asleep, exhausted from shouting, by the time they'd found him.

"Quick! Come down!" Andy's voice sounded a long way away. She lowered herself carefully, till she felt Andy's hands grip her waist. "You can let go of the rope," he said. Jen hoped he might hold her a little longer, but Andy's mind was on treasure and nothing else.

As he let her go, Jen turned to look around the stash. All her life she'd heard stories from the old guys in Dark Cove about the rum-running days. Ships would come close to shore, unload the rum at night and slip away. They hid the rum here in this stash until it could be shipped to American ports. The way Jen heard it, rumrunning was dark, dangerous work, dodging American patrol boats all the way.

The stash smelled damp and musty. "What's so exciting?" asked Jen. Her voice echoed weirdly.

"Look." Andy shone his light around the square room. "It's amazing – they must have lived down here. They had a table and chairs, and a ladder." He put one foot on the ladder's lowest rung. It fell away, soft with age and rot.

A broken chair lay on its side. There were rusty old bedsprings and moldy mattresses. Empty crates were stacked on one side like a kind of cupboard. Jen shuddered. "People talk as if the rum-running was yesterday but it was a long, long time ago, Andy," she gulped, "We're not going to find anything here. Let's leave."

"I guess you're right, there's nothing here." Andy was shining his light in every corner. "I was hoping they might have left something – like a strongbox full of money."

"Wouldn't they have come back for it?" Jen asked.

"Maybe they got caught and went to jail and could never get back. It might be worth digging some holes in the floor …"

"Some other time," Jen said. "Right now, I want to get out of here. This place gives me the creeps and your aunt Maggie will be wondering what happened to us."

"I'll bet there's buried treasure somewhere on this island," Andy muttered under his breath. "Imagine if I could find it – get rich, like Paul Speers. Then you and Kel could have your horses, and Dad wouldn't have to work underground way up north and keep changing jobs –"

"What are you mumbling about?" Jen tugged on his sleeve. "Come on, start climbing." She shoved him toward the dangling rope.

◆◆◆◆◆

Minutes later, hurrying to the farm, Jen and Andy met Kelsie racing down the path to find them.

"It's settled!" she cheered. "Paul Speers is crazy about the island. He calls it 'a jewel from the past.' He wants to help us rebuild the barn, and buy hay for the horses for the winter."

"Your Aunt Maggie agreed we can keep all four of them?" Jen gaped at Kelsie. "What changed her mind?"

Kelsie threw up her arms. "Paul was so full of ideas for fixing up the farm it was contagious. She loves the idea, as long as we do all the work."

"And Mr. Speers puts up all the money?" asked Jen. She noticed that Kelsie was already calling him 'Paul.'

"It's not a problem for him – he's rich." Kelsie linked arms with Jen and danced her down the path. "He's got big plans for his stud farm. He'll be going in front of the town council in a couple of weeks to get them approved."

"What plans?" Jen gave her an alarmed glance. "I thought he was leaving everything at the farm exactly the same."

"Well, he has to make *some* changes." Kelsie turned to Andy who was lagging behind. "What did you find in the smugglers' stash?"

"Nothing," said Andy glumly. "An old table and chairs and some empty crates."

"What did you expect? Wads of thousand dollar bills lying around?"

"Don't be stupid …" Andy's voice trailed off. Aunt Maggie and Paul Speers had caught up to them. They were walking arm in arm.

"Horses on Saddle Island again," Aunt Maggie was saying. "It will be just like when I was a child."

"Now, all we have to do is get Gabriel Peters to ferry the horses across to the island," Kelsie sighed happily. "I'm sure he will."

◆◆◆◆◆

But she was wrong. When Kelsie tracked Gabriel down that evening, he was washing the deck of his Cape Islander boat, the *Suzanne*, at the Peters' dock.

Kelsie's heart beat so fast at the sight of his dark curly hair and welcoming grin that she had a hard time explaining what she wanted. "Isn't it great?" she finished. "If you help us get the horses to Saddle Island we can get Caspar healthy again, and save Zeke and Midnight and Sailor from the canners."

Gabe kept hosing down the deck while he listened. "How can your Aunt Maggie afford all those horses?" he asked.

"Paul, Mr. Speers, promised to help –" Kelsie started to tell him.

"Wait a minute." Gabe cut her off. "I don't want anything to do with a scheme of Speers'." He shot a stream of water close to Kelsie's feet.

"Stop that!" She jumped back. "Why not?"

"My dad doesn't trust him. Thinks he's full of hot air." Gabe's father was a town councilor in Dark Cove. "Dad's going to vote against his plan for Harefield Farms."

"But why?"

"I already told you. He has big city ideas, but –"

"Stop!" Kelsie was furious. "Just because Paul Speers is from Boston doesn't mean he can't have good ideas for Dark

27

Cove." She was worried as well as angry. If Paul didn't get his plans approved he'd be so disappointed. He might give up. Kelsie knew what it felt like to have your dreams squashed by narrow, suspicious people. She hadn't thought Gabe was one of them.

"I don't see why you don't like Paul." She tried again. "If you weren't so narrow-minded, you'd see he's just what this stuffy cove needs."

Gabe turned away with a scowl. "If you think Dark Cove is so stuffy, why don't you –"

"I know what you're going to say. If I don't like it here, why don't I just leave?" Kelsie hopped off the *Suzanne's* wet deck. "Well, I'm not leaving this town. My family's been here as long as yours, and I don't mind if things change in Dark Cove, and I trust people even if they do come from somewhere else."

As she marched back down the Peters' dock, Kelsie tried to swallow her rage. How could Gabriel not like Paul? Had he even talked to him?

She felt Gabriel's hand grab her shoulder. "Kelsie, I didn't mean I want you to go." When she turned, his dark eyes were laughing at her. "But you're like a short fuse on a stick of dynamite. Once you start burning with an idea you don't stop till it blows up in your face. Why do you have to be so stubborn and horse-crazy?"

Kelsie might have melted if he hadn't been laughing. As it was, she shook off Gabe's hand with a shrug. "Don't worry," she said. "I'll find another way to get the horses across to the island."

But as she stalked away, Kelsie had no idea how to do that. First, she told herself, Jen and I need to go up to Harefield Farms and make sure *our* horses are ready to travel.

# Chapter 5
# Free Horses

As Kelsie and Jen biked past the "Sold" sign at Harefield Farms the next morning, they saw a strange pickup parked in the yard.

"That must belong to the stableman Mr. Speers hired to look after the horses." Kelsie hopped off her bike and leaned it against the barn wall.

Harefield Farms looked rundown and deserted, and the stableman turned out to be a gloomy stranger who grunted a greeting when they said hello and then went back to hauling hay.

Zeke was in crossties in the center of the barn. "I hope that stable guy's taking good care of the horses," Jen murmured, stroking Zeke's soft brown nose. "Zeke didn't even nicker when he saw me, as he usually does." The nervy brown horse stomped around in the crossties, tossed his head, and expressed his disapproval with every twitch of his muscles.

Kelsie slipped into Midnight's stall. "Midnight's been cribbing – she never did that." Midnight was a Canadian mare, black and sturdy, with a thick wavy mane and tail. The top of her stall door was wet and shredded from chewing on the wood.

"I wish Mr. Speers had hired us to look after them –" Jen started to say.

Just then, the stableman stuck his head in the barn door. "Hope you kids don't have a notion of goin' for a ride," he grumbled. "I just got these horses cleaned up. And watch the pony. He bites."

Kelsie glanced over at Sailor's stall in horror. What was happening here? The little Newfoundland pony had never bitten before. He was a lovely red bay, with a reddish head and shiny white body, a black mane, tail and four black stockings. The smallest kids had ridden him when Harefield Farms was giving riding lessons, and he never bucked or shied, let alone bit anybody.

"How much exercise do the horses get?" asked Kelsie.

The stableman shrugged. "Not my job to exercise them – just feed and water them regular." He pulled his baseball cap down over his eyes. "I got to get in that stall there, if you're finished."

Kelsie gave Midnight a carrot from her pocket, and she nibbled it gratefully from her hand. "We've got to get these guys out of here," Kelsie muttered to Jen as she left the stall. "This is no life for a horse."

"How are we going to do that if Gabe won't take them?" Jen followed her to the barn door. "The Peters' boat is the only boat around here that's big enough to ferry a horse to the island."

"I know that." Kelsie grabbed her bike. "I wish I hadn't fought with Gabe – it's just that he made me so mad." She glared back into the big open barn. "I get steamed up so fast. Just now, I wanted to scream at that stableman, and it's not his fault the horses aren't exercised."

Jen hopped on her own bike. "Maybe if you apologize, Gabe might change his mind."

"I hate to back down," Kelsie stormed, "but I guess it's worth a try."

◆◆◆◆◆

Scuffling her feet down the Peters' dock later that day, Kelsie wondered what she would say to Gabriel. Would he even talk to her? She remembered how he'd glowered when she called him narrow-minded.

Gabriel wasn't on his boat. The *Suzanne* rocked gently at its mooring, like a boat without a care in the world.

Kelsie stood and let the ocean wind blow through her hair. She took a deep breath of the salty air. That felt better.

A deep voice behind her made her spin around.

"Looking for me?"

"Gabriel – you scared me!"

"Wasn't trying to." He was carrying two large bait buckets, one piled on the other. He set them down and looked at her with his laughing dark eyes. Kelsie took another breath. No use thinking about those eyes, or Gabriel's wide shoulders, or the way his shirt, rolled up past his elbows, showed off his muscles.

"I came to say I'm sorry."

"Oh?"

"And to ask you again about taking the horses over to Saddle Island." Kelsie pushed on. "Jen and I were just up to see them. They need to get out of that barn."

"Hold up." Gabriel held up his hand to stop the rush of words. "Speers was here a little earlier."

Kelsie held her breath.

"He offered me three hundred dollars to ship the horses to Saddle Island." Gabriel hoisted the bait buckets again and swung them onto the deck of the Suzanne. "I told him I wasn't interested in his money."

"You weren't?" Kelsie gulped.

"No. I told him he could keep his credit card in his pocket." Gabriel's eyes had an angry glint in them now.

Kelsie felt her heart sink. She could picture the scene. Paul wouldn't realize how insulting he was being – talking as if Gabriel's precious lobster boat was some kind of barge for hire.

"So, I guess –" she started.

" … And then your brother came along." Gabriel straightened up and smiled at her. "It seems he has his own reasons for wanting to hang out on Saddle Island – asked me if I'd help you and Jen get the horses to the island so you three could spend serious time there for the rest of the summer."

Kelsie groaned to herself. Andy and his crazy treasure hunt. She hoped he hadn't told Gabe. He'd think her brother was an idiot.

"I told him I'd do it as a favor for a friend." Gabriel shrugged. "And that we'd better go while this fine weather holds." He glanced up at the clear blue sky. "We should start early tomorrow morning so we don't hit those rocks when the tide goes out. Would that suit you?"

Now Kelsie couldn't speak. The words stuck in her throat. "To-tomorrow will be good," she managed to gasp at last. "Thank you, Gabriel."

"Thank your brother." He gave her a lopsided grin.

◆◆◆◆◆

Kelsie dashed to the Clam Shack to give Jen the news. From the Peters' dock on the far side of Dark Cove, a path led up and down the rocks. Small houses in bright colors clung to the rocks like toys flung on a crazy quilt. There were vegetable gardens in shallow dips in the rock, flowerbeds and lobster pots and the hulls of old dories.

The Clam Shack where Jen and her mother worked was a restaurant and gift shop, perched a little above the other houses where the road started to climb out of Dark Cove, up the steep hill to Harefield Farms and then on along the coast.

Jen was setting the tables with napkins and silverware when Kelsie burst through the door. Jen's mother, Chrissy, called from the kitchen where she was frying clam strips. "Jen, can you take that order?"

"It's just Kelsie, Mom," Jen called back.

Kelsie grabbed the rolled up silverware from Jen and started to help. "Guess what?" she said breathlessly.

"I know." Jen blushed as she gathered ketchup and vinegar bottles from a shelf to put on each table. "Andy was in here earlier. He told me Gabe will take the horses for us. Your brother can be pretty persuasive when he wants to be."

"For once, I agree," Kelsie laughed. "I can hardly believe it, Jen. They're going to be ours – Zeke and Midnight, Sailor and Caspar. Saddle Island will be horse heaven."

"It'll mean a lot of work …" Jen paused and frowned. "And I still have to help Mom here in the restaurant."

"Andy will give us a hand – especially if *you* ask him," Kelsie teased.

Jen blushed again. "You shouldn't use me to manipulate your brother."

They both turned as the door opened and Paul Speers stepped in. "Hi, girls. Andy just told me the good news."

At the sound of his deep voice, Chrissy Morrisey appeared in the kitchen door, wiping her hands on her cook's apron. Her cheeks were flushed and her hair, fine like Jen's, was in wispy curls from the heat of the fryer.

"What's the news?" she asked.

"Gabe is taking Mr. Speers' horses over to Saddle Island for us tomorrow, if the weather's okay." Jen turned back to the tables and arranging the ketchup.

"They're going to be your horses," Paul Speers reminded her. "Not mine anymore."

"But he's paying for all this, aren't you, Mr. Speers?" Jen lifted her small chin and looked directly at the tall man.

"Sure." He smiled. "No problem."

Kelsie would have liked to strangle Jen. How rude! What was wrong with her?

◆◆◆◆◆

Meanwhile, Andy was down at Gabriel's dock.

Gabriel was clearing the *Suzanne's* deck, preparing the fishing boat to transport the horses the next day. Everything loose had to be tied down, stowed under hatches or put ashore. He'd ferried Caspar from Saddle Island to the mainland two weeks ago, but Caspar had been too exhausted to cause any trouble. That was a lot different than ferrying four frisky horses that had been shut in a barn too long.

"Ever hear any stories about pirates around here?" Andy asked, fishing for information.

Gabriel stopped coiling rope and grinned down at him.

"Oh, there're lots of stories. Some of them pretty wild. People say that pirates used to put in at Saddle Island to get fresh water and repair their ships before they headed off across the ocean. It was one of their favorite stopping places."

"Did they have treasure on those ships?" Andy asked, trying not to sound too interested.

"That's what I hear." Gabriel nodded. "Gold and jewels

they stole from other ships. And they'd sometimes stop along these shores to bury it if another ship was chasing them."

Andy jumped up from the dock and leaped aboard the flat rear deck of Gabriel's Cape Islander. "Let me help you with that rope," he said. "So pirates *might* have buried some treasure on Saddle Island." He squinted up at Gabriel. "That would be even better than smugglers' loot. Want to be my partner and look for it?"

Gabriel laughed. "I'm too busy fishing for green treasure – the kind with claws. Some day, I want to come back with a million dollar's worth of lobsters in this boat." He patted the *Suzanne's* hull lovingly, and then frowned. "I hope those horses don't do her any harm tomorrow."

# Chapter 6
# Trawler Transport

"Andy, can you ride Sailor down to the Peters' dock this morning?" Kelsie raced into Andy's room the next morning and bounced on the end of his bed. There were two small rooms with slanted ceilings upstairs in Maggie Ridout's blue house. They each had a bright rug on the floor, lovingly hooked for them by their aunt. Andy's had a pattern of a boat on a blue sea, Kelsie's the head of a white horse. Aunt Maggie slept downstairs in a closed-in sun porch.

"Me? Ride?" Andy blinked open his blue eyes. "You know I don't –"

"Please? Sailor's just a small pony," Kelsie pleaded. "Even little kids can ride him."

"Is that why you want me to ride him? Because I'm short?" Andy grumbled.

"Don't be crazy. He's good for a beginner, that's all. We really need you. Jen can't handle three horses."

"Where will you be?" Andy wrinkled his nose at her.

"I'll be bringing Caspar, from our barn." Kelsie took a deep breath. "I hope he makes the trip all right." Caspar had made good progress in the three days since the vet had seen him, but he still had a cough.

"Please, Andy," she begged her brother. "If you can ride a bike you can ride a horse." Kelsie knew this wasn't true, but if he rode the pony he'd be safe enough. "Jen will show you," she added slyly. "She's a good teacher."

"Oh. Well, maybe I could try," Andy said.

◆◆◆◆◆

"How do you get on one of these?" Andy called to Jen. He was trying to jump on Sailor's back from the ground.

"Wait. Let me help." Jen hurried to his side, leading

Midnight and Zeke. "You have to put your left foot in the stirrup, and then swing your right leg over."

Jen held Sailor's reins while Andy tried to get his foot in the stirrup. He managed to heave himself into the pony's saddle.

"Whew. I made it," he started to say. Then, as Sailor started to walk away, a shocked look spread over his face. He grabbed for the front of the saddle. "He's moving!"

"I thought you liked speed." Jen was trying not to laugh as the pony broke into a jog.

"Sure, I do, when I turn on the motor!" Andy yelled. "This guy moves on his own."

"He's a horse, not a motorboat." Jen giggled. "Stop kicking him with your feet—he thinks that means GO!"

"How do I make him stop?"

"Sit back, say 'Whoa' and tighten your hands on the reins," Jen told him.

"I should never have said yes to this," Andy hollered, hauling on Sailor's reins. "How does Kelsie talk me into – whoa, Sailor."

The pony looked over his shoulder, his fuzzy forelock covering one intelligent brown eye. Then he stopped. The look of fear faded from Andy's eyes.

"Just stand still while I get Zeke tied on behind Midnight," Jen called.

Riding down the road to the cove at a trot a few minutes later, Andy bounced up and down, laughing. "This … is fun," he called to Jen.

"Good!" Jen shouted back. She was glad Andy was on Sailor, who knew how to take care of a novice rider. Zeke, now, that would be a different story. The leggy brown horse was so full of pent-up energy from being shut in a stall that it had been hard to tie him on, and he was fighting the rope every step of the way.

◆◆◆◆◆

Kelsie tossed the bow rope on the *Suzanne's* front deck. She watched Gabriel in the wheelhouse spin the wheel and ease the Cape Islander gently away from her mooring.

On the wide back deck, Jen braced her legs, holding a horse's lead rope in each hand.

"We've got four or five hours to get all the horses to the island without risking my boat on the rocks," Gabriel shouted to Kelsie over his shoulder. "I'll come back for the other two as fast as I can."

There had been no trouble loading Midnight and Sailor. They had clomped onto the swaying, bobbing deck like pros. They were used to Jen and trusted her. If she said a boat was a good place to be, they believed her.

Kelsie hoped Caspar would be the same. He'd been too tired the night they rescued him to cause any trouble on Gabe's boat, but the big horse had been a problem loader in the past, kicking and fighting to avoid getting into a horse trailer. What would he do when he had to step off the solid dock and onto the *Suzanne's* wobbly deck?

Andy stood on the dock beside her, holding Zeke. The brown horse had a look in his eye that said he'd had about enough of being dragged around. Andy kept jerking on his lead rope and that didn't help.

"Do you want to hold Caspar, instead?" Kelsie asked. "He's pretty quiet."

"All right. My arm's getting sore." Andy reached over to take Caspar's lead rope as Kelsie let go.

This was just the chance that Caspar had been waiting for. He threw up his head, jerking the rope out of Andy's hand, and swung around, almost knocking Kelsie into the water. In a flash he was clip-clopping down the dock, onto the shore and heading for the beach.

"Andy!" Kelsie screamed. "Why did you let him go?"

"I didn't – it wasn't my fault."

"Hold Zeke. I have to go after him."

Kelsie left Andy gripping the nervous horse and jumped from the dock, trying to head Caspar off. He mustn't go in the water! She'd never catch him and the cold water might put him back days.

She tore down the beach after her horse. "Caspar, stop!"

But Caspar had no intention of stopping. He was heading for the sea.

Kelsie saw a lean figure stride down the shore, step into Caspar's path and fling out her arms. Caspar stopped, surprised, just long enough for a wiry arm to grab his halter and pull him firmly to a halt. It was Aunt Maggie, in her loose sweater and baggy pants. "You wretched beast," she scolded Caspar. "Don't you know when you're well off?"

"Thanks, Aunt Maggie," Kelsie gasped. "I guess … I guess he's feeling better."

"Good enough to get into trouble." Aunt Maggie narrowed her eyes. "I came to see how you were getting along. Is that Andy, all by himself on the dock holding a horse? Where's Speers? I expected to see him here."

"I don't know. We didn't see him at the farm. He must be away, on business …," Kelsie's voice trailed off. The truth was, she'd expected to see Paul Speers today, too. She wondered if it had anything to do with Gabe, and Gabe's father. Was he angry because they were against his plans?

◆◆◆◆◆

Aunt Maggie stayed with them until Gabe came back with the boat an hour and a half later.

"No problems," Gabriel told Kelsie, as he swung the *Suzanne* into her mooring. "As soon as Sailor and Midnight saw the fresh grass they settled down like they'd always lived on an island. Jen stayed with them."

Kelsie beamed. "That's great news."

"It's Caspar you have to worry about," Andy muttered to Gabe. "He just made a break for the beach."

"I'm sure Caspar will be fine, too, once there are other horses on Saddle Island." Kelsie glowered at her brother. "Come on, let's get him loaded." She didn't want Gabriel to think Caspar was going to be any special trouble, but of course, Andy had to tell.

Aunt Maggie held the *Suzanne's* bow rope while Gabe leaped ashore to help load. "Caspar first," he decided.

Taking a deep breath to steady herself and the horse, Kelsie leaned into his side, blocking his escape route down the dock. "Come on, Caspar," she soothed, "It's not scary. Just like stepping into a trailer. Come on, you've done it before. Remember? It was easy." She talked to him with every step, until he was safely aboard the boat.

"Here, Gabe." She handed the lead rope to him. "Keep a good grip while I get Zeke."

"You're pretty good with horses," Gabe said, but he had spoken too soon.

Zeke had no intention of following Caspar meekly onto the deck. He put up a fierce fight. He reared and plunged and kicked out with his back legs as they tried to get him aboard.

"He's going to kick my hull to pieces!" Gabriel shouted. He was still holding Caspar's rope.

"No. Ugh. He'll be – fine." Kelsie finally got Zeke shoved to the far side of the deck. She grabbed Caspar's rope. "Get the boat started," she roared at Gabriel. "Get away from the dock so he won't try to jump back on it." If the horse managed to get free and fell between the boat and the dock, he could be crushed.

Gabriel dived for the wheelhouse. Seconds later, the engine started with a roar. Aunt Maggie heaved the bow rope to the deck and the *Suzanne* swung out into the cove.

"What about me?" Andy hollered from the dock.

"Get your boat and come to the island," Gabriel shouted back. "I'll have to bring the *Suzanne* back to the Cove and the girls will need a ride."

Kelsie, meanwhile, fought for control of Zeke. "You behave yourself," she whispered furiously. "You've got the captain mad at you."

Zeke responded by lashing out with his hoofs. To her horror, Kelsie saw he had left two dark dents on the Suzanne's perfect turquoise hull.

Gabe had heard the THUD! He turned with a scowl on his handsome face. "If he does that again," he yelled, "I'll feed him to the fish."

◆◆◆◆◆

"So typical!" Andy raged to Aunt Maggie as they hurried back along the shore to the Ridout dock. "Kelsie gets me to help because she knows I love Gabe's boat and then I DON'T EVEN GET TO GO."

"Big sisters can be a blight," Aunt Maggie agreed. "Your grandmother, my big sister Elizabeth, was exactly like your sister Kelsie. Same auburn hair and green eyes. She used to get me to do all the things she didn't like to, like gutting fish."

"Did she?" Andy exclaimed. He'd never known his grandmother – even the memory of his mother who had died two years before, was fading. "What else did she make you do?"

"Hit the fish we caught over the head to kill them." Aunt Maggie laughed. "She loved fishing, she just didn't like what happened to the fish after she caught them."

She nodded. "And just like you, I was always trying to keep my big sister out of trouble. She had the craziest ideas."

"Like Kelsie!" Andy exclaimed.

"Exactly like Kelsie. So, you have to promise me you'll keep an eye on her out there on Saddle Island. Don't let her run away with her hare-brained ideas."

"I'll try," Andy promised. He didn't say anything about his own plans for the island – searching for treasure. Aunt Maggie was likely to think that was hare-brained, too.

"Let me help you load up your boat," Aunt Maggie was saying. "I have something special to show you."

# Chapter 7

# Hidden Cave

"Take these." Aunt Maggie handed a pair of shiny wood oars to Andy. "If your boat gets stuck in the passage at low tide, you can pull up the motor and row."

Row? He'd never row a boat if he could help it, Andy thought. Were these oars "the special thing" she wanted to show him? "Those are gr-great," he stammered, feeling as if his aunt's piercing gray eyes could see right through him. "They look new."

"They are new. I ordered them from Steve Murphy. He used to make wooden boats for all the fishermen around here." Aunt Maggie paused. "I ordered them when I saw how much you liked your dad's old boat."

Andy stroked the smooth, varnished wood. Handmade oars must have cost Aunt Maggie a lot. "Thanks," he said. "How do they work?" The oars were smooth, all the way down. No oarlocks.

His aunt reached under the edge of the skiff and yanked on a string. Two wooden pins popped up. "Thole pins to hold the oars," she said briskly. "They can be pushed down for hauling nets over the side."

"Cool." Andy pushed the pins back down. "But I'll try not to get stuck by the tide." Aunt Maggie didn't realize that he'd been fooling around with boats all his life. Every town they'd lived in had been on a big lake. He'd always had a motorboat, always fished with his dad. Okay, maybe it wasn't the ocean, but a boat was a boat.

Andy stowed the oars along the sides of the skiff. He started the engine and waved goodbye to his aunt.

Aunt Maggie waved back. She watched as the skiff headed out across the calm sea. "He looks so much like his father in that boat," she murmured to herself. "A new generation of our family on Saddle Island – it's like a miracle." She had brought up her nephew, Douglas MacKay, Andy and Kelsie's dad, after his parents drowned when he was thirteen. She had been sad when Douglas left Dark Cove at eighteen and moved far from the sea. And now with Andy, zooming across the water in his green boat, it was almost as though he was back. Aunt Maggie's heart thumped painfully in her chest. "Please be careful!" she whispered to Andy, even though she knew he couldn't hear.

◆◆◆◆◆

Andy's skiff chugged past Fox Island, a long skinny strip of land closest to Aunt Maggie's dock, past tiny Teapot Island, and across the passage to Saddle Island, the biggest of the three. One good thing about this whole messed-up morning was that now he got to be alone. This was the perfect day to explore the outer side of Saddle Island.

It was already after ten. He leaned forward, wishing the boat could fly faster. Wouldn't it be great if he could find treasure and help Dad and Aunt Maggie out of their money troubles?

Andy turned the throttle to full speed and zoomed around the island's southern end. There! The open ocean stretched in front of him. Still flat, still calm, but how huge and blue. Andy could picture whales under his hull, sails appearing over the horizon. This was where the pirate ships cruised, with their cargoes of gold and silver and jewels. Andy could picture them sparkling in a chest, overflowing.

He turned sharply to the left to search Saddle Island's shoreline for any sign of a pirate landing place. Steep rocks fell to the sea with no beaches in this section. The trees on top were stunted by the wind.

He slowed his motor to a crawl, a steady putt-putt-putt.

Suddenly, Andy realized he was not alone. Just off to the right of the bow, a face was watching him. The face had bright eyes in a shiny bald head, a pointed nose with whiskers. It looked straight at him as if to say, "Ha! You didn't expect to see me here, did you?"

Before Andy had a chance to wonder who or what the face belonged to, it disappeared in a blink.

A few seconds later it bobbed up again on the other side of his boat, and closer. Andy leaned over to look. Now he could see a sleek black body under the surface. It dived and was gone again.

"A seal!" Andy exclaimed out loud. It was the first time he'd seen one. Maybe if he shut off his motor, the seal would come right up to the boat.

He cut the engine and the boat rocked gently over its own wake. Andy sat perfectly still. There it was again. But this time behind the boat, and swimming for shore. Andy started the motor. The skiff swung around.

The seal was heading for the shore, no doubt about it. Andy followed. At the base of the cliff under an overhanging rock was an area of dark shadow. As he motored closer, the seal disappeared again. Where had he gone this time?

Andy peered at the shadow again. Could it be? It was. The mouth of a cave. The seal had guided him right there. Andy turned the throttle to its lowest speed and glided into the darkness of the cave.

◆◆◆◆◆

"Look what that fool horse did to my boat!" roared Gabe, seeing the full extent of the damage for the first time. They were moored on Saddle Island, with Caspar and Zeke tied to trees.

"This is the last time I carry horses on the *Suzanne*!" Gabe raged. "I hope they like it on this island because they're never going to leave."

Unloading had been worse than loading, even with Jen's help. Zeke had let go with a major dump on Gabe's clean deck. There were nicks on the rails where the horses had stepped and Zeke's kick marks all around the hull.

Gabe's face was flushed. "When my dad sees this … I wish I'd never agreed to such a crazy idea. This is a lobster boat, not a barn. It's Pop's pride and joy – he keeps it cleaner than my mom's kitchen floor and look at that." He pointed to the pile of horse manure.

"I'm really sorry," Kelsie apologized. "We'll help you fix it up."

"Have you got tools? Have you got paint?" Gabriel groaned. "I can't fix the *Suzanne* over here. I've got to get back to the Cove."

"If you have a bucket," Jen said timidly, "we could at least clean the poop off the deck."

Twenty minutes later, after swabbing the deck, Gabe took off, still looking mad enough to strip eels. Kelsie gulped, "He didn't even wish us luck."

"We're going to need it, too." Jen looked around the landing place. "I wish Andy would get here."

"You talk as if my brother was any use," Kelsie grumbled. "All he can think about is searching this island for treasure. It's such a crazy idea – I know he's going to get us into trouble."

"Come on, he rode Sailor all the way down to the dock, didn't he?" Jen hurried over to untie Zeke's lead rope from the tree. "And he isn't the first person to go treasure hunting around here." She stroked Zeke's glossy side. "But we can't wait for him. These guys need water. We should take them to the spring and get them set up with the other horses."

They headed for the ruins of the farm, leading Caspar and Zeke.

"You're going to love it here," Kelsie whispered to Caspar. "I can't wait to ride you around the island. And I've got a really great plan for you and Midnight. But first, you have to get totally better." She could still hear a slight wheezing as he walked.

◆◆◆◆◆

Once inside the low cave entrance, the noise of Andy's outboard engine, magnified by the rock walls, was deafening. He turned the control to STOP.

Silence enveloped him like a shell.

Okay, he'd try his new oars. He pulled the string on his

left side. The two thole pins shot up with a thud ten times as loud as before. Andy tried fitting an oar between the pins. It felt awkward. The creak of the oar, the splash as he dipped it in the dark water, the thump of his feet on the skiff's wooden planking, all echoed around him.

It took him a long time to get the feel of the oars, get them working properly.

"This place is huge," Andy breathed. He turned his boat so he was facing into the cave – he took a small flashlight from his life jacket pocket, turned it on and clamped it between his teeth.

Now he could see. There was space above him, space beyond the boat, lit dimly by the flashlight. The arch of the entrance behind him was a slice of blue light, reflecting the water.

Andy rowed cautiously backwards, deeper under the cliff. Slowly, very slowly. Was the ceiling getting lower, or was it just his imagination?

At the back of the cave there was a ridge of pure white sand. A ledge of rock stretched from the sand under the surface of the water. Andy rowed closer to the sand, beached the skiff and stepped out.

The sand was deep and soft. He took a few steps, stopped and shone his light ahead. In its narrow beam he saw something sticking up out of the sand. It looked like a piece of bleached wood.

Andy plunged closer. Shone his light again. What he thought was a chunk of wood had horrible gaping eye sockets and huge teeth.

It was the skull of a large animal – a horse?

In his shock, Andy dropped his light. Then he must have stepped on it because the light blinked out. Andy fell to his knees, fumbling for it. He searched in the darkness for a long time, but by now he'd stirred up the sand so much he knew it was impossible to find it.

He swung around to look back at the entrance. It was a narrow crescent of light. Hadn't it been bigger when he motored in? Was the cave that deep?

All at once an icy chill shot through Andy's whole body. The tide! He had forgotten the tide. It was rising when he left the shore, it had been rising the whole time he was in the cave. It could rise so high the whole entrance would be underwater.

"Cripes! How could I be so stupid?" Andy swore, and his voice echoed back at him. He'd only lived by the ocean for six weeks but already he'd seen how the rising and falling tides changed everything. He could get stuck in here. The sea could fill the entire cave and he'd drown.

He plunged back through the fine sand to the skiff, frantic, feeling his way, trying to go as fast as he could.

There – he had it. Andy shoved the boat with all his might out into the black water of the cave and leaped awkwardly aboard. Panicked, he struggled to find the oars. One of them slipped out of the pins and splashed into the water. He'd never find it in time. Already the crescent of light at the cave entrance filled completely each time an ocean swell rolled in.

Andy scrambled for the back seat, yanked the starter cord with every scrap of strength in his body. "GO! GO! GO!"

The motor fired up with a cloud of choking smoke.

Andy couldn't see. He pulled the throttle arm hard and the skiff spun on its flat bottom, tipping dangerously. Twisting the control to top speed he roared ahead, trying to escape through the narrowing entrance.

The smoke clouded his view. For a split second, Andy had a vision of striking the rock with a splintering crash. He would go down with its wreckage. He flattened his body, as low as he could, still clinging to the motor. It roared in his ears as the rock closed around him.

The skiff shot out of the entrance, into the sunshine. The roaring of the engine stopped. Andy lifted his head and looked back at the cave entrance. It was just a dark slit above the water. He had cleared it by a hair.

"Close one," Andy muttered. He sat, rocking in the skiff for a long time, watching the tide rise right over the cave's mouth. He'd left one of his new oars back there. It would get washed out to sea. Aunt Maggie would never forgive him for losing it.

There was a chance that the oar was still inside the cave,

would end up on that ledge where he'd found the skull. It was a perfect place to hide something … like pirate treasure. He'd have to go back and look – when the tide was low.

Andy was shivering as he reached back and pulled the starter cord once more, heading for the other side of the island. Jen and Kelsie must be wondering where he was.

# Chapter 8
# View From the Cliff

"Jen, Kelsie, where are you?" Andy called, as he stumbled up to the ruined barn on Saddle Island.

"Trying to clear this barn out, as if you cared." Kelsie straightened up and shouted back. "We *needed* you. Where have you been?"

The two girls were clearing the last of the weeds and fallen roof timbers out of what had once been a small stone barn. There had been a fire and the roof had caved in, years ago.

Andy jumped over the doorsill and bent over, panting, resting his hands on his knees. "I came as fast as I could – ran all the way from the shore. I found something – an underwater cave."

Kelsie shoved her thick curls out of her eyes and wiped her sweaty forehead. "I don't care. It doesn't matter what crazy treasure hunts you go on or what amazing discoveries you make. Paul Speers is going to help us rebuild this barn and buy hay for the winter."

"So you don't want to hear about what I found?" If Kelsie was going to act like this, he wouldn't even tell her about the horse's skull, Andy thought.

"No, I don't want to hear about it." Kelsie picked up a piece of wood and chucked it dangerously close to Andy's head.

There was a moment of silence, then Jen stripped off her work gloves and walked over to Andy as if announcing which side she was on. "Tell *me*," she said. "I've never seen a cave on this island. Where is it?"

"On the outer shore." Andy shot a triumphant glance at his sister, then turned back to Jen. "Down near the south end of the island where the cliffs are high. I could only see a bit of it because the tide was in, but when it goes out, I'll bet you could get right inside." He'd already decided not to tell Kelsie or Jen about almost getting caught by the tide in the cave.

"You took a big risk," Jen said, "taking the skiff out there. The waves crash in on that shore something fierce."

"Not today," Andy said. "It was pretty calm."

"Still, you should take my kayak the next time you want to explore that cave. It's a lot safer." Jen was peering at him as if she guessed he'd been in some kind of trouble.

"You'd let me take the *Seahorse*?" Andy brightened. A kayak would be perfect for getting deep inside, right to the back, as far as you could go. He could look for treasure … might even be able to find the missing oar with a kayak.

"I'll give you a few lessons, first," Jen promised.

"Thanks. I know there must be something in there –" He was going to tell Jen about how the seal had led him into the cave when Kelsie interrupted with an angry snort.

"Shut up, Andy. I'm sick of hearing about your dumb adventures. What's the matter with you, Jen? Why are you listening to him? We've got work to do here."

Jen threw down her gloves. "Nothing's the matter with me," she said. "And you don't have to talk to your brother like that, or throw things at him, either."

Kelsie glared at her. "Don't you care about the horses?"

"Of course I care." Jen threw back her head. "I just don't like being bossed around. Finish clearing the barn yourself."

She marched off, with Andy right behind her.

Kelsie watched them go. She stood, rigid, inside the four barn walls. Jen! What was she thinking? Taking off with her useless brother like a kid, playing a game.

She stumbled to the barn door, not even looking where she was going. "How am I supposed to look after three horses and a pony by myself?" she wanted to shout. I thought Jen was *my* friend – I thought she cared about Caspar and Zeke and Sailor and Midnight as much as I do.

Tears stung her eyes and she swiped them furiously away.

Kelsie could see the horses in the old pasture beside the barn. Caspar was nose to tail with Zeke on a line strung between two trees. The big white horse still needed constant watching, and Zeke couldn't be trusted. The two horses seemed to be enjoying the warm sun, but they needed to move, not just stay tied up.

Nearby, Midnight was grazing on good green grass, while Sailor frisked from one end of the old pasture to the other. If only they had a fence, she could set Caspar and Zeke free, too. Then they'd be like a real herd, a small band of horses with water and grass and space.

Kelsie gave herself a shake. She'd make it happen. She marched to the spring at the end of the pasture, bent and gazed at her reflection in the dark pool. She saw her curly hair fanned around her face. Her pale eyebrows knotted in a frown. Her straight nose, tight mouth – just like Aunt Maggie's! Startled by the resemblance, Kelsie rubbed her hands across her mouth, then tried to smile at her image in the pool. "I wish," she said out loud, " I wish I could show Jennifer and Andy I can handle these horses all by myself. That I don't need either of them. Don't care if they drown, looking for treasure."

Suddenly she shuddered. Her own grandmother had drowned in the ocean near here, along with her grandfather, leaving her dad an orphan at thirteen. Drowning wasn't a wish you made on Saddle Island, no matter how mad you were. "I take it back," she whispered, "but I wish they hadn't run out on me like that."

A horse came up behind her and nuzzled her shoulder. At first Kelsie thought it was Caspar – that was one of his tricks – but when she turned to look she saw a black nose and a frosted black mane. Midnight. "Thank you," Kelsie said, stroking Midnight's cheek. "Thanks for reminding me what all this work is for. I'm going to train you to pull with a harness, if you'll let me. That's what your ancestors used to do, pull sleighs in the winter and carts in the summer and logs out of the woods. And maybe I'll train Caspar too. A pure black and white team. You'll look great."

Kelsie threw herself back on the soft grass, full of horse dreams.

◆◆◆◆◆

"We shouldn't stay away long," Jen called over her shoulder as she and Andy raced up the trail towards the end of the island.

"But I want to show you my favorite place. I haven't been there for weeks. I used to come almost every day."

"Why?"

"You'll see. You'll love it." Jen grinned at him, and then blushed. She and Andy were hardly ever alone and she liked him, a lot. She hoped he liked her, too. She felt badly about fighting with Kelsie – she was the best friend Jen had ever had – but sometimes she was too rough on Andy.

Jen pushed ahead along the old road that ran up the west edge of the island. Moss-covered rocks lined the path where settlers long ago had tossed them to clear the road. The trees were covered in moss, and they hung low over the trail. A salt tang from the ocean filled the air. It felt like a magical place.

"This way …" Jen showed Andy a narrow path that led upwards. "It's not as steep as it looks."

But the route up the cliff called the Saddle Horn was a tough climb and Andy was puffing when they reached the top. He reached out to grab for Jen as she threw her legs over the edge and perched on a narrow ledge high over the sea.

"Watch out!" he cried. Sea birds soared below them. The blue water was far, far below.

"It's safe." Jen laughed at him. "Come and sit beside me."

Andy choked back his fear. He carefully climbed down to sit next to Jen, his spine pressed against the rock. "Great view." He wasn't sure if his heart was pounding so hard because he was terrified, or because he was sitting so close to Jen.

"You're braver than Kelsie." Jen laughed. "She wouldn't come down here. But you look like you're going to faint. Your face is as white as a sheet. Come on. We don't have to stay."

She stood up, fearlessly, and grabbed Andy's hand. He wriggled around until he was facing away from the sickening drop and let her help him back to the cliff top.

"See," Jen was saying, "the whole island is spread out down there, like a map. There's the farm, and farther down the landing place, with your green skiff and –" She stopped. "Andy what's the matter? Do you still feel faint?"

"N-no." Andy shook his head. "But look. Way down at the

end of the island …" He pointed. "Can you see that funny green line that runs from the shore to the middle of the island?"

Jen nodded. "I see. The trees are a darker color."

"Why would they be darker?" Andy swung to face her, his blue eyes round with the question.

Jen shrugged. "I don't know. Different trees? Younger trees? Maybe somebody cleared a strip a long time ago, and then it grew back in. What's so exciting? There're lots of old roads and paths on this island."

Andy was back staring at the view from the cliff. "I think that strip leads right to that cave I found." He started down the path from the cliff. "I want to go and see close up. C'mon."

Jen glanced at her watch. "We don't have time," she finally called after Andy's disappearing blond head and green shirt. "It would take the rest of the afternoon and I have to get back to the Cove to help Mom at the Clam Shack."

# Chapter 9
# Stalled Plans

On the way back to Dark Cove in the skiff Andy was silent. All he could think about was getting back to the cave and then exploring the strange green strip he'd seen from the top of the cliff. They must be connected somehow.

Kelsie was quiet, too. "She's supposed to be my friend," she fumed to herself, staring at Jen in the front of the skiff. "How could she choose Andy over me and the horses?"

Jen perched on the prow of the skiff, one leg draped over either side, staring straight down into the water. The tide was flowing out. Soon the causeway rocks would stick up like black teeth, but right now, the worst danger was that Andy's propeller would strike one just under the surface.

"More to the right!" she shouted back to Andy.

The boat swerved violently. Jen held on tight to keep from being flung into the ocean.

"You'd better raise the propeller," Jen gasped. "I almost didn't see that one in time."

"We could row if we had more than one oar." Kelsie glanced at the shiny new oar along one side of the skiff. "Where did you get that, Andy? And where's the other one?"

"Never mind," Andy grunted.

Just then, there was a scraping jar and the boat jolted to a stop.

"We're aground on a rock," Jen said. "I'll move back and maybe we'll float free."

Holding both sides of the skiff, Jen swung to the middle of the boat. She picked up the oar and pushed hard against the rock. It didn't budge forward or backward. The skiff just spun in a circle.

"Let's all get in the back," puffed Jen. She and Kelsie squeezed in beside Andy. The bow shot into the air. Jen poled with the oar, and with a horrible grating sound, the skiff slid off the rock and floated free.

"Phew!" Andy exclaimed. "Another few minutes and we'd be high and dry on that rock." He wanted to throw his arm around Jen and hug her, but he didn't dare.

"We're not past the last of them, yet." Jen flipped back her fine brown hair. "Start the motor and go slow. I wish we had the other oar – we could row."

Andy swung the propeller back into place and turned the throttle to its lowest speed. Jen clambered back to the front of the skiff and lay across the bow, pointing with her hands to direct Andy past the rest of the rocks.

When they were clear, she flipped onto the front seat and grinned back at Kelsie and Andy. "Made it!"

"Do you think we hurt her, running aground like that?" asked Andy anxiously.

Jen ran her hand over the old wood planks at her feet. "She doesn't seem to be leaking," she said. "She's a nice little boat. Why haven't you given her a name, Andy?"

"Yeah," Kelsie added. "You usually name everything you own, from your bike to your favorite tee-shirt."

"Don't know ..." Andy blushed. He twisted the throttle arm and the motor burst into noisy thunder. The skiff had a name. It was the *Jennifer*, but that was his secret.

At Aunt Maggie's dock Jen jumped out of the boat and tied it to the float. "Let's take a look in your Aunt's fish house," she said. "Maybe we can find another oar in all that junk she keeps in there."

Andy quickly tied the stern with another rope. "Good idea." There was a chance Aunt Maggie wouldn't notice one of the new oars was missing, at least not right away.

"Coming, Kel?" Jen swung around to ask her.

Kelsie was still sitting glumly in the center of the boat. "No. Go ahead. Have fun in the fish house." She couldn't keep the sarcasm out of her voice.

As they raced up the dock to the old shack, Andy had a chance to ask Jen, "Can you come back to Saddle Island tomorrow?"

Jen nodded. "I'll bring the kayak."

"Think we could go look at that funny green strip we saw from the Saddle Horn?"

"I can't," Jen said. "I want to patch things up with Kelsie. I should help her with the horses."

"She shouldn't act so … bossy." Andy glanced at Jen as he tugged open the fish house door. "She's bossed me around my whole life. But she's supposed to be your friend."

"She doesn't mean it." Jen waded into the piles of old fishing gear stored in the neglected building. "It's just that she's so wrapped up with Caspar. Look. There's an oar in the corner."

Andy helped her wiggle the old oar out from under an eel basket. "It's not in very good shape," he said doubtfully. "It's all cracked and the paint has worn off."

"It'll do in an emergency," Jen told him. "Let me take it down to your boat. I have to talk to Kelsie. Alone."

◆◆◆◆◆

As she stowed the oar in the skiff a few minutes later, Jen put her hand on Kelsie's arm. "Kel. I want to say I'm sorry – for leaving you – and going off with Andy. You think it's two against one, but it doesn't have to be – it can be the three of us, together."

Kelsie grabbed Jen's hand. "Well, I'm sorry I said you didn't care. I know you care. It's just that I –" She wanted to say she hated it when Jen chose Andy over her, but the words wouldn't come out.

"It's okay," said Jen smiled. "Friends?"

"Friends." Kelsie said with a grin. She straightened her shoulders. "Can you do me a favor? If Paul Speers comes to the Clam Shack tonight, call me. I want to ask him when he's coming over to the island to build a fence for the horses."

"All right." Jen bit her lower lip. "He's there almost every night. You'd think he'd be getting pretty sick of clams by now. I'll call you as soon as he comes in."

She hopped out of the skiff and headed up the dock at a run.

Kelsie climbed out of the skiff and went inside to set the table for dinner. Aunt Maggie didn't accept help with cooking, but she liked Kelsie and Andy to set the table and do the dishes.

Tonight she'd made macaroni and cheese. It was delicious, but Kelsie noticed that her aunt just picked at her food.

"Aren't you feeling well, Aunt Maggie?" she asked.

"I'm fine. Just a little tired." Her aunt smiled and passed her hand over her forehead. Kelsie remembered looking in the wishing spring and seeing her Aunt Maggie's face reflected back at her. They both had the same high forehead. It was just that Aunt Maggie's was so lined, especially when she was tired.

After dinner, while Andy went down to inspect his skiff for damage, Kelsie wandered around her aunt's garden, thinking about the horses, alone on the island.

The sky looked like rain. What if they were out on the picket line in a storm all night? They'd be so wet, and cold. Kelsie was already used to the sudden changes of weather along the Atlantic shore. Dry weather was unusual, wet more likely. That's why her mother had never wanted to come back to Nova Scotia, Kelsie thought suddenly. Mom hated rain.

Kelsie shoved the memory of her mother away. She'd died two years before and Kelsie tried not to think about that time. Her mom had been from Sydney, on Cape Breton Island. That's where she'd met their dad, Douglas MacKay, when he was a young miner. Dad had often talked of bringing his family back to Dark Cove to visit his aunt Maggie, but somehow they never had, till now. Kelsie thought that was likely because of Mom. She'd say, "The East Coast, that damp, drab place, I never want to see it again."

But Kelsie thought it was beautiful, even in the rain. She wished she had Caspar there to comfort her at that moment. She'd hug his big head and tell him her troubles and he'd make her feel better.

Just then her Aunt Maggie appeared in the back door, the phone in her hand. "It's Jen. For you."

Kelsie hurried across the yard to take it.

"Paul Speers is here." Kelsie could barely hear Jen over the rattle of dishes in the background. "He's stuffing his face with onion rings and fried clams."

"I'll be right over." Kelsie handed the phone back to her aunt. "I'm going to the Clam Shack for a minute," she told her. "I want to ask Mr. Speers about the fence for the island."

"Well, while you're at it, ask him when he's coming to fix the roof on the barn," said Aunt Maggie. "It looks like rain again – we'll have to put the buckets back."

"I will," Kelsie promised, and raced out the door.

Paul Speers had a good table, she saw as she came in the Clam Shack. It was by the window, overlooking the Cove. There was hardly anybody in the restaurant, and Jen's mother was talking to Paul, leaning toward him, one hand on her hip.

Shouldn't she be in the kitchen? Kelsie thought. I have to talk to Mr. Speers about that fence.

But as she overheard snatches of their conversation, Kelsie realized this wasn't a casual talk, and she couldn't just barge in and interrupt.

"Why don't you leave this dead-end job and come and work for me, at the farm?" he was asking. "You could be my secretary, farm manager, whatever you liked. Help me get ready for the town meeting in a couple of weeks."

"I'll think about it." Chrissy Morrissey shrugged and smiled.

Just then, Kelsie caught a glimpse of Jen's pale face through the glass panel in the kitchen door. Jen was watching her mother and Mr. Speers, too.

"What's he saying?" she asked urgently, as Kelsie swung through the door.

"He just offered your mom a job," Kelsie said. "Manager – at Harefield Farms."

"I was afraid of that," Jen groaned. "He's been buttering her up since he got here."

"But wouldn't a manager's job be better than being stuck in here frying fish?" Kelsie gestured around the small, steamy kitchen.

"Sure. If it was a real job," Jen shot back. "But you don't understand. Jobs like that just don't come up in Dark Cove."

Kelsie thought she did understand. "You're so used to things closing and shutting down around here that you cling to what you have, even if it's bad," she said. "You're all like Gabe, afraid of change. The places I've lived, mining towns, there's always new stuff happening. Nobody's afraid to take new jobs –"

"Yeah? Like your dad and his great new job in the diamond mine?" Jen shook her head. "Sorry. I'm sorry. I didn't mean to throw that up to you. But I'm just afraid my mom isn't thinking clearly. I think she's dazzled by Mr. Speers. I've heard him in here – promising everything to everybody. In the few days he's been here he's got half the town *dazzled*. What if he isn't for real?"

"I guess it's about time we found out." Kelsie stared at Jen. "We need fence posts and wire and tools on the island."

"And somebody to help us dig fence postholes," Jen added. "The three of us can't do that."

"Right. And fence post holes." Kelsie agreed. "Okay. If you can think of a way to interrupt that conversation out there, I'll see if Mr. Paul Speers is going to come through for us."

"I know how to get Mom's attention." Jen smiled her mischievous upturned grin. She turned up the deep fat fryer and tossed in some fresh breaded clams. "It'll just take a few minutes."

They waited, watching the hot fat bubble, until an acrid fishy smell filled the room.

Jen threw open the door. "Mom! The clams are burning," she shouted.

◆◆◆◆◆

The burning clams worked like magic. Jen's mom came rushing back to the kitchen and Kelsie grabbed the chance to talk to Mr. Speers. Before he left the Clam Shack, he had promised to meet them at Harefield Farms tomorrow morning. And he was going to help them get a fence for the horses.

That night, as she lay in her narrow bed under the slanted ceiling, Kelsie dreamed of horses romping in a green field, of riding Caspar down a leafy lane to the south of the island, of swimming on his strong back into underwater caves. She woke with a start. Could you really swim a horse into a cave? she wondered sleepily.

# Chapter 10
# Salvage

"Here you are, kids. All the fencing you can use. Help yourselves."

Kelsie, Jen and Andy peered through the doorway of a small shed behind the barn at Harefield Farms the next morning. Heaped inside were coils of white wire and small cardboard boxes.

"I don't know what Harefield was planning to do with all this fence, but I don't need it," said Paul Speers. He threw the doors wide. "I'll get the stableman to truck all this down to the dock for you."

Kelsie stared at him. "This is the wire for an electric fence," she said. "But there *is* no electricity on Saddle Island."

"That's what these are for." Speers pulled some flat black plates from one of the boxes. "Solar panels. Electricity from the sun. All the instructions are in that box, and I'll bet Andy is pretty good at putting things together."

"What about fence posts?" Jen gaped at him.

"You'll figure that out. String the wire on trees, if you have to. Look kids, I'd love to help you with this project, but right now I've got a lot of work getting my stud farm proposal ready for the town meeting. Think this will tide you over until we can get a crew on the island to build a proper fence?"

"Sure. Uh … thanks, Mr. Speers," Kelsie managed to say, still gazing at the coils of wire.

"And salvage anything else you want from the barn," Speers added. "Tack, grooming supplies, feed, anything you need." He waved his hand airily.

"Seriously?" Kelsie asked.

"Sure. I'm clearing the whole place out, and you might as well have it. Fill up the whole truck with whatever you like. Sorry, got to go now."

With a final wave, Paul Speers roared away in his silver Mercedes.

"Well." Kelsie watched the car disappear. "He *did* come through, sort of."

"Oh, sure." Jen gave a scornful shrug. "Electric fence? Trees for posts? Solar panels?"

"Andy *can* make it work," Kelsie told her. "He did a whole project on solar energy when we lived in the Yukon – won first prize at the science fair."

"You did?" Jen asked Andy.

He blushed as he picked up a heavy white coil and lugged it to the stableman's pickup. "Kelsie helped," he said.

Kelsie shoved another bundle of wire into the truck bed. "We're a good team, when we work together. I've got a deal for you Andy. If you'll help with the fence, I'll stop making fun of your treasure hunt. I might even help."

"Deal." Andy grinned.

"Good. I'll check the barn," said Kelsie. "See if there's more stuff we need."

Minutes later she was hoisting saddles off racks, heaping bridles, lead ropes, and grooming kits onto a wheelbarrow. A few birds chirped from the rafters over her head and the place still had the sweet smell of horses and hay. But the big old barn seemed empty and quiet with no horses.

"I can't believe we can take all this stuff." She was panting as she wheeled it to the truck. "There are bags of feed, too, and I found some draft harness for Midnight. I want to train her to pull. Canadian horses are famous for that."

"How am I going to get all this over there?" Andy groaned, as the pile in the back of the pickup grew higher.

"Lots of trips in the skiff?" suggested Jen.

"Let's get started." Kelsie looked from one to the other. "The sooner we get those horses fenced, the better."

❖❖❖❖❖

The pile of gear, unloaded on Aunt Maggie's dock, looked like a small mountain.

"We can't take all this," Andy protested. "The skiff will sink!"

Just then, Gabriel came down the dock.

As he strolled towards them, Kelsie felt her heart pound and her palms get sweaty the way they usually did when she saw Gabe. She wished he didn't churn up her feelings like this.

"What have you got here?" Gabe asked. He wore that maddening half grin that made Kelsie think he was laughing at her. She threw him an angry look and a shrug. None of his business.

"Stuff from Harefield Farms," Jen explained. "Electric fence and other stuff. Mr. Speers said we could take anything we needed from the barn –"

Andy cut her off. "We have to get it all to Saddle Island," he said. "I know Zeke kind of messed up the *Suzanne* yesterday, but could you help us?"

"Gabriel doesn't have to help," Kelsie sniffed. "We can manage by ourselves."

Gabriel was looking over the bags of feed, tack, harness and grooming kits. "Why is Speers giving you all this?" He narrowed his eyes. "Won't he need it if he's getting new horses in the barn?"

"He's generous, and helpful. Why are you so suspicious?" Kelsie glared at Gabe.

He raised his dark eyebrows. "I don't trust the guy. And I don't want to see you kids get hurt."

"There it is again!" Kelsie thought furiously. He thinks of us as little kids. Maybe Andy and Jen were kids but she was old enough to feel – Kelsie shoved the thought of all she felt for Gabriel to the back of her mind. Right now he was just annoying.

"We'll get Mr. Speers' stuff to the island in Andy's skiff," she insisted. "We wouldn't want to contaminate your precious lobster boat."

"Whatever you say." Gabriel gave her a fatherly pat on the shoulder, turned, and strode away.

"*Kelsie*!" Andy hissed furiously. "What have you done? This is going to take us all day."

"He's only trying to help." Jen shook her head. "Why do you get so mad at him?"

Kelsie was still feeling a storm of emotions, watching Gabe disappear up the dock. Her cheeks stung as if they'd been slapped. "He's just so sure he's right about Mr. Speers," she burst out, "and he's wrong."

# Chapter 11
# Ride to the Treasure Pit

For the next two weeks Kelsie didn't see Gabriel Peters, except from a distance, and there was too much happening on and off Saddle Island to dream about his hunky good looks or the way he made her feel.

Every morning she and Andy headed for the island in the skiff, with Jen paddling the kayak behind. Their first job was to build a fence. Strung from tree to tree to make a roughly rectangular pasture, the electrified wire didn't give the horses a bad shock. They could feel the charge when they got close and that was enough to keep them away.

Once Caspar was free to run from one end of the pasture to the other, with other horses for company, he got better, just as Kelsie had hoped. He was so bursting with energy she was afraid he might try to escape from the pasture. At Harefield Farms, he had jumped fences, busted out of pens, even figured out how to work the latch on a stall door – each time galloping straight down to Dark Cove beach for a swim in the ocean. She kept her eye on him for any sign that he might be plotting his escape from the pasture.

While Caspar continued to improve, Kelsie started training Midnight to pull in harness. Midnight seemed to understand the whole procedure, from getting the breast collar on to having a log fastened behind her. She actually seemed to enjoy pulling.

It was horse heaven – everything that Kelsie had dreamed of. The four school horses that had worked so long and hard at Harefield Farms had a free life, with good grazing, fresh water and plenty of freedom. And soon Caspar would be well enough to ride.

She and Jen spent every day with the horses, and only the gloomy clouds hanging over Dark Cove kept them from being perfectly happy. Jen worried about her mom, who had taken the job with Paul Speers. Aunt Maggie constantly fretted about money, and there was no news of a job from Kelsie's and Andy's dad.

Andy had been waiting for a chance to get back to the underwater cave he'd found and look for treasure. He was afraid to take the skiff inside again, and he had to wait for Jen to show him the way to the strip of green trees they'd seen from the Saddle Horn. In the meantime, he had been taking kayak lessons every day to prepare for going back in the cave.

"I saw Aunt Maggie scraping the bottom of the flour bin to make pancakes for breakfast," he said one morning, as they were mooring the skiff and the Seahorse on Saddle Island. He looked up at the two girls and asked, "Do you think we could go take a look at that cave on the far side of the island?"

Kelsie threw him a look. She knew Andy hadn't given up his idea of finding buried treasure on the island.

"Not today." Jen brushed her fine hair out of her eyes. "It's too windy to take the kayak out in the open ocean." She pointed to the waves tossing in the passage between the islands. "But we could go look for that dark green strip we saw – see if it's an old road."

"Great!" Andy yanked the skiff high up on the rock and tied it securely. "I'm sure the road is linked to the cave, somehow. Let's go."

"We can get to the south end of Saddle Island faster if we take the horses," said Kelsie.

"You mean ride?" Andy's eyebrows shot up. He hadn't been on Sailor's back since the ride from Harefield Farms to the dock.

"You did great before." Jen grinned. "Come on. We'll take the trail down the eastern shore of the island. On horses it'll take a couple of hours, instead of half a day."

"All right." Andy hoisted a pack of drinking water and food from the boat. "I guess it's a good idea."

"It's a great idea!" Kelsie said. She didn't mind treasure hunting if she could do it on a horse.

They hurried up the trail from the boat landing to the farm to get the horses.

A few minutes later they were saddled up and ready to go. Kelsie on Midnight. Jen on Zeke. She'd settled down the tall brown horse by doing groundwork and riding him around the pasture every day.

Andy stroked Sailor's cheek. "This is going to be fun, right?" he murmured. The Newfoundland pony swiveled his ears forward to listen. He had a handsome head, with deep cheeks, a narrow muzzle and wide-set, intelligent eyes. His ears were short, furry and very expressive.

Jen came to help. "Remember how to mount?" she asked.

"Sure. Foot in the stirrup, swing my leg over and don't kick his sides till we're ready to go." Andy climbed aboard.

It wasn't graceful, Jen grinned to herself, but at least he looked like he knew he was riding a horse and not sitting on a bike seat.

Meanwhile, Kelsie was saying goodbye to Caspar, over at the wishing spring. "I know what you're wishing," she whispered. "You hate to get left behind. I'll soon be riding you again, but not quite yet."

Caspar tossed his white head as if to disagree.

"Oh, all right," Kelsie sighed. "I'll tie you behind Midnight, but don't get any funny ideas of jumping in the ocean."

They set off, with Jen and Zeke in the lead, Andy and Sailor in the middle and Kelsie and Midnight bringing up the rear with Caspar tied behind. Zeke set a quick pace. Soon they were heading down the overgrown road at a slow trot. "Watch for low-hanging branches," Jen called over her shoulder to Andy.

"Won't bother me," Andy muttered, "I'm on a low-hanging horse." It was true. Sailor could zip under branches where Jen had to duck.

There were still blackberries hanging from vines along the old road, and every so often Sailor would stop to rip some off with his strong teeth. "You shouldn't let him eat," Kelsie said, as Midnight almost collided with Sailor at one of his sudden stops.

"Why not? I would eat too, if I could reach the berries."

"It's not good discipline for Sailor. He's got to know who's the boss."

Andy laughed. " He knows, all right. *He* is."

Kelsie could see this was true. Andy's legs and arms flapped in all directions. She doubted if he had any contact with the bit in Sailor's mouth. Sailor was just doing what he liked, going where he wanted. Kelsie had seen kids of six ride that pony better than her brother.

She could see Andy turn to the sea as they came out of the trees along the cliff top. The surf was pounding in today, throwing spray high in the air. At high tide, it would reach the top of the cliff and when it did, the path they were on would be slippery and treacherous.

Andy jerked on the reins. "Whoa, Sailor!" he yelled.

"What are you stopping for?" Kelsie rode up beside him. Andy's face was scarlet with excitement.

"Right here – this is where I saw the seal and found the cave." He rode closer to the edge.

"Come back, you idiot!" Kelsie urged Midnight forward, caught up to Andy and bent low to grab Sailor's reins. "What are you trying to do, ride Sailor over the cliff?"

"I'm trying to see the cave."

Jen had circled around and joined them. "We'll have to get to the cave at low tide on a calm day," she told Andy. "No way to reach it from here."

"Well, let's look for the road, then." Andy's hair seemed to be standing on end, he was so excited.

"There's a small cove just up ahead." Jen pointed. "Maybe that's where it starts."

They rode down a steep, rocky slope to a groove in the rock that was almost choked with driftwood logs and twisted spruce trees.

Here, they got off their horses. The ocean pounded in on a rocky shore to their left, the land rose steeply to their right.

"These trees can't be from the pirate era," said Kelsie. "They aren't much taller than my head."

"They could be hundreds of years old." Jen ran her hand over the spiky needles. "They don't grow fast because of the wind."

"Stunted, like me," Andy murmured.

Jen grinned at him. "You're not that short."

They climbed the slope. If it had been an old pirate trail, all signs had been wiped away. The only clue was the spruce trees, growing so close together it looked like they had been planted. As they pushed the horses farther from the shore, the trees grew taller, sheltered from the fierce wind off the Atlantic.

"I don't think there's anything here," Jen said, struggling to push through the dense tangle of branches. "Sorry, Andy."

"Let's go back to the path along the shore," shouted Kelsie. "This is too thick for the horses."

But Andy ignored them. Sailor was leading *him*, now, pulling on the lead rope. The pony didn't seem worried by the thick brush.

He headed for a big gray boulder as high as his shoulder.

"Whoa! What are you doing?" Andy protested.

Sailor yanked the rope out of Andy's hand with a twist of his head. He sidled up to the rock and rubbed against the rough granite as if it was a scratching post.

"You miserable …" Andy swore, bending over to pick up Sailor's rope.

Then he saw something that made him straighten up and shout, "Kelsie! Jen! Come here! Look at this."

They scrambled through the brush, leading Midnight, Caspar and Zeke.

"A rock?" Kelsie stared at him. "That's the big excitement?"

"Get down and look underneath. It's sitting on three smaller rocks, like a table on legs. And it's shaped like an arrow, pointing straight ahead." Andy's words tumbled over each other. "Sailor found it. There's stuff like this in the books about pirates. Marker rocks."

Jen was gazing at him with a doubtful frown.

"Don't you get it?" Andy threw up his hands. "It's a sign we're on the right track."

Jen handed her reins to Kelsie, got down on her hands and knees and looked under the boulder. "He's right." She straightened up and pushed back her fine hair. "Someone, or some thing, picked up this big rock and balanced it on three little rock legs."

"Are you sure?" Kelsie asked. "It looks like it's been this way forever."

"Well, four hundred years is practically forever," Andy said, smoothing his hand over the boulder's surface. "The trees have grown up around it, but I'll bet this pointed rock was put here as a marker."

He urged Sailor away from his comfortable scratching and pushed forward in the direction of the arrow.

Kelsie and Jen followed, Kelsie with a rope in each hand.

After twenty minutes of hot, hard going, Jen stopped to wipe her forehead. "We must be getting near the middle of the island," she gasped.

Kelsie groaned. "It's all a big wild goose chase. Come on, we'd better keep up with Andy or he'll get lost out here."

But Sailor's whinny told them Andy was just ahead. They found him at the foot of a tall spruce, looking down at a shallow depression in the ground.

It was full of rounded stones.

"I'll bet this is a pit where the pirates hid their gold," Andy exclaimed. "We found it!"

"Those are beach stones," Jen pointed out. "Look how they've been polished by the waves."

Andy said in a low voice. "They brought the stones up from the beach to fill in their hole. That's what the road was for."

Caspar was tugging on the lead rope, shaking and bobbing his head. There was a wild look in his eye.

"What's the matter?" Kelsie handed Midnight's rope to Jen and went to soothe her agitated horse. "What's wrong, Caspar?"

# Chapter 12
# Speers' Plan

"Caspar doesn't like it here." Kelsie stroked his quivering side. "There's something he's afraid of."

"How do you know that?" scoffed Andy.

"Look at him. He acted like this when we first found the smuggler's hideout. If we'd taken one more step we would have fallen in, but Caspar wouldn't let us." Kelsie looked closely at the ground. "We should be careful. There's danger here."

They all stood silent in the strange clearing, looking at the pit full of stones.

Andy started to explore the clearing, kicking at strange mounds around the shallow hole. "It doesn't matter," he said. "We're too late."

"What are you talking about?" asked Jen.

"We're not the first ones to find this place." Andy's disappointment was written all over his face. "These mounds are dirt piles they dug out of the pit. The gold's probably all gone."

Kelsie shook her head. "Maybe you're right about someone digging," she said, "but don't you think if they'd found the treasure on Saddle Island, we'd know about it? Aunt Maggie's never mentioned anything like that."

"It could have been dug up before she was born," Andy argued. "These dirt piles are old – look, they're covered in weeds and bushes."

"I agree with Kelsie." Jen shook her head slowly. "People in Dark Cove have long memories and there's no such thing as a secret around here. If somebody even a hundred, or two hundred years ago found buried pirate treasure on this island, it would still be the talk of the Cove."

Andy's face brightened. "Maybe they tried, and failed," he said slowly. "Maybe it's still down there. I have to come back with a pick and shovel – tomorrow."

"But we'll have to be careful," Kelsie warned. "Caspar's

warning us that there's something bad about this clearing, and horses don't lie."

♦♦♦♦♦

"I can't come and help you dig," Kelsie told Andy at breakfast the next day. "I just remembered today's the meeting where Paul Speers presents his plans for Harefield Farms. I want to find out what happens and be there to support him." She wondered if she'd see Gabriel at the meeting. The thought made her heart race.

"Fine. Jen and I will go without you," Andy announced. "We'll take the horses."

Kelsie looked up quickly. Her brother had tossed that off as if he and Jen would rather go without her. "Take the horses?" she said sarcastically. "You've been riding exactly twice in your life and you talk like a cowboy."

He flushed to the roots of his hair. "I'm getting along with Sailor real well," he muttered.

After Andy left to meet Jen, Kelsie ran up to her room to get ready for the meeting. In case she saw Gabe, she took special care to brush her hair back from her face and fasten it with a clip at the back. She thought it made her look older. She put on her favorite blue sweater and best jeans and smiled at herself in the mirror, glad she was so tall. With makeup she could look sixteen. Even without, she looked at least fifteen.

Aunt Maggie called up the stairs. "If you're ready, I want to drive up to Harefield Farms and see Paul Speers before the meeting."

Kelsie pounded down the narrow stairs, anxious to get to the town hall to see Gabe. "Are you sure we should bother Mr. Speers at home?" she asked her aunt. "He'll have so much to think about, with his plans for the farm and everything."

Aunt Maggie was pulling on her baggy cardigan. "I want to find out when Speers plans to fix my barn roof and whether he's ordered enough hay for all your horses for the winter, like he promised," she said. "If we wait till we get to the town meeting, we might not have a chance to ask him." She put her arm around Kelsie's shoulders and gave her a squeeze. "You might as well come with me."

As Aunt Maggie drove slowly up the winding road to the farm, Kelsie wondered again why everyone, including her aunt, was so suspicious of Paul. Just because he was rich, didn't mean …

At that moment, Kelsie realized something was wrong with the familiar view of the farm beyond the gate. "Aunt Maggie," she gasped, as the car jolted to a stop, "where's the barn?"

A cloud of dust rose from where a bulldozer was leveling the ground.

"He tore it down!" Kelsie gasped. "The barn is gone."

Aunt Maggie's lips were pressed tightly together. She got out of the car and stared at the remnants of the barn. "So this is how he protects his precious heritage site," she muttered. She got back in the car and slammed the door. "I wonder what the town council will have to say about this."

Kelsie couldn't speak. Now she knew why Mr. Speers had let them take everything they wanted from the barn. He was going to tear it down to the ground. The old building wasn't beautiful, but it could have been rebuilt, restored. But there was no way you could restore a heap of rubble!

◆◆◆◆◆

At ten-thirty, the Dark Cove Community Hall was filling up quickly. As Kelsie and Aunt Maggie took two vacant seats on the aisle, she could see Gabe in the front row. His father, Guy Peters, and the other councilors sat at a table, facing the crowded hall. Gabe's father was an older version of Gabriel, shorter, and thinner, with stooped shoulders and thinning hair.

Kelsie tried not to stare at Gabriel, tried not to notice how adorably his dark hair curled around his collar. Tried to remember that he and his father wanted to stop Paul Speers in his tracks. That might mean the end of all their plans for the island. At the same time, the horrible image of the bulldozer, erasing the remains of the Harefield Farms barn, flashed before her eyes. How could Mr. Speers have done that?

Just then, Paul Speers strode down the aisle. Instantly, he was the center of attention in the room, although people tried to pretend they weren't looking at him. He was wearing a gray suit. A suit – in Dark Cove! He took a seat just across the aisle from Kelsie.

There was a lot of boring business to get through before the question of his plans for the stud farm came up. Kelsie sat in a stew of confusion, not wanting to look at him, not knowing what to think.

Then Mr. Peters called his name.

Paul Speers made his way to the front of the room, briefcase in hand. Smiling, he hooked up his computer for a PowerPoint presentation. It was slick and well-organized, showing a beautiful horse farm spread out across the top of the cliff with an indoor riding ring where the barn had been, a racetrack and endless expensive white fencing.

"I'd just like to say," he hit the pause button, "that I was sorry to tear down the original barn at Harefield Farms. I was advised that the foundation was unsound, and the building was a hazard."

Kelsie felt Aunt Maggie poke her in the ribs. "What nonsense!" she hissed.

"The new barns will be safer for the horses," Paul Speers went on. "The old one, with no sprinkler system and the hay stored above the stalls, was a fire trap."

"Humph," Aunt Maggie snorted. There were restless stirrings in the crowd. Kelsie glanced at Gabriel. The back of his neck and his ears were red. He must be furious about the barn – he hated change.

The councilors were speaking. Kelsie tried to concentrate, but it was hard with Gabriel in view.

One councilor didn't like the size of the new house Speers planned to build. "It's ten times the size of any house in the whole Cove."

Gabriel's father worried about the road down the cliff to the house. "I think we're going to have erosion problems there."

Someone from the audience stood up and said that Speers' new farm was the biggest building project since the fish plant closed in Dark Cove, and that everyone needed the work.

Someone else said the jobs wouldn't last and in the meantime the look of the whole cove would be wrecked.

Kelsie could see Paul Speers start to lose his patience. "I bought this land to build a breeding farm for champion racehorses," he said briskly. "I'd like to get on with the job."

But in the end, they voted against him and his plan.

Kelsie jumped to her feet as he as he strode down the aisle toward her. "Mr. Speers –" she started to say.

He brushed past her with barely a glance. "Sorry, I don't have time now."

Kelsie stood staring after him.

Behind her, Gabriel had come up to talk to Aunt Maggie. Kelsie swung around. "What's going to happen to those horses now?" Aunt Maggie was saying.

"I'm sorry if it causes a problem for you and the kids," Gabe answered, "but I'm glad we stopped him."

"I'm sure Mr. Speers will help with the horses," Kelsie blazed. "Just because he got turned down doesn't mean he'll go back on his promises."

But as people filed out of the hall, Kelsie saw Paul Speers jump into the silver Mercedes and speed away. When would he be back to prove she was right about him, and everyone else, especially Gabe, was wrong?

◆◆◆◆◆

On the south end of Saddle Island, Andy and Jen were taking a lunch break.

"What a wasted morning," Andy grumbled. "We've worked for hours, and all we've done is lug beach stones out of this pit. We haven't even started to dig." He threw the plastic wrap from his sandwich into the strange hollow at the center of Saddle Island.

"Don't pollute," Jen scolded. "Just because you're mad."

It was a hot day, with no wind. Zeke and Sailor were tied to trees nearby, out of the sun.

"Sorry!" Andy scrambled to retrieve his bread crusts. "But let's go look at the cave, instead of digging. Maybe there's a tunnel that leads from the shore to this treasure shaft."

"If it is a treasure shaft." Jen stood up and stretched. "Look, Andy, the tide's already turned. By the time we ride to the landing, get the boats and motor around to the cave it will be too dangerous to go inside."

"We can just zip in and zip out," Andy begged. "It won't take long in the kayak." He jumped up, crumpling his sandwich bag. "Let's get going."

On the way back, Jen rode behind Andy. She noticed that his legs weren't flopping at Sailor's sides. He wasn't bouncing up and down like a kid on a trampoline, either. If he kept up like this, he'd soon be ready for a bigger horse – maybe Midnight. Jen saw he didn't yank on the reins every time Sailor tossed his head, or treat the pony like a firecracker about to explode. Good signs. It would be wonderful if Andy started to like horses. Then they'd really have something in common.

Jen found herself picturing the two of them, she riding Zeke, Andy on the black mare, galloping side by side.

Just then, Sailor made a sudden sideways move and Andy flew in the opposite direction. He landed hard, on his rear end.

"Ow! You miserable four-legged monster," Andy howled at Sailor, who stood looking at him from under his forelock as if he wondered what Andy was doing on the ground.

"It wasn't his fault." Jen realized she'd been too confident of Andy's riding ability. He still needed to learn some basics of staying on a horse. She hopped off Zeke's back and helped him up. "Are you all right?"

"Sore!" Andy blushed and rubbed the seat of his jeans. "And I feel stupid."

"Can you get back on?" Jen asked. "I'm worried about the time. We should take the horses back to the farm and forget the cave."

"I'm fine," Andy said quickly. He climbed back on Sailor to prove it. "I really want to get there today." Aunt Maggie hadn't noticed the missing oar. She seemed too tired to spend any time down at the dock these days. But it was only a matter of time till she discovered it was gone, and then she'd be so disappointed in him. Wouldn't it be great if he had a handful of treasure to show her instead – then they could buy all the oars they wanted.

# Chapter 13

# In the Cave

When Jen and Andy reached the landing place, Jen unsaddled Sailor and Zeke, led them over to a grove of trees, and tied them where they could graze.

"I forgive you for tossing me off onto the rocks," Andy muttered in Sailor's fuzzy ear. "But next time, give me a little warning."

"We'd better go." Jen took a look at the rising water. "I'll tie the kayak behind the skiff. You drive."

The *Seahorse*, on a long rope, bounced over the skiff's wake like a long red bug as they rounded the point. Andy leaned forward in the bow, searching for a landing spot near the cave. To his right, under the overhang of rock, the entrance was a yawning mouth.

"Take her in there." He pointed to the small, tree-choked cove they'd visited before. It wasn't far from the cave entrance and would give them a safe place to tie up the skiff and launch the kayak.

In no time they had the skiff securely moored. But as he slipped over the seaweed-covered rocks to untie the kayak, Andy shuddered, remembering the terror of being almost trapped by the rising tide on his first visit to the cave.

Jen looked at him strangely. "What's wrong? You look like you'd just seen a ghost."

"I guess," said Andy, "it would be awful to get stuck inside the cave, with the tide coming in."

"Go fast," Jen warned. "And when you get in the cave, don't fool around. Have you got your light?"

"Right here." Andy patted the pocket of his life vest. "I wish you had a kayak for two," he said. "I'd like you to come with me."

Jen sighed. "A double-seater costs a lot of money. I'm lucky to have even this one." She patted the *Seahorse's* hull.

Andy remembered Jen's lessons as he waded into the water, holding the kayak with two hands. Struggling to stay balanced, he lifted one leg into the cockpit, then the other, and lowered himself carefully, so he didn't tip. He felt for the foot pedals and leaned back to take the paddle from Jen.

"Okay," he said breathlessly. "I'm ready."

Jen gave him a light shove and he was off, paddling along the cliff face towards the cave entrance. Dip, swing, dip, swing. Left, right. Left, right. It was quiet in the kayak, after the noisy motor. The ocean swell rolled against the rock with a low boom and a sigh.

"Remember," he heard Jen shout behind him as he steered the kayak into the cave entrance, "Don't stay too long."

Andy went from bright sunlight to sudden dark. As his eyes adjusted he could see he was speeding toward the back of the cave. Better slow down. He didn't want to crash Jen's kayak against the rock. He stopped paddling and dug out his light.

He could see the drift of white sand, as pure and fine as the sand in a fish tank. Saw the skull of the horse with its hollow eyes sticking out of the sand. Below it, the flat ledge was now out of the water. He shone his light around the ledge looking for the gleam of an oar. Nothing.

Then Andy saw something that made his blood race. Into the rock, right in front of him, someone had pounded an iron ring. A place to tie up a boat.

Up until that moment, in the back of his mind, Andy hadn't really believed in the pirate legends. Searching for treasure had felt like a kind of fantasy game. But now …!

Andy steered the *Seahorse* closer to the ring. He reached out and felt it – cold and wet and hard into the rock. This was real. If it wasn't pirates who had brought their boats into this cave and tied them to this ring, who could it have been?

He'd promised Jen to zip in and out, but he just *had* to explore further.

Andy focused his beam of light along the cave's back wall. He couldn't be sure, but it looked like there was a small cavity to the left. Could it be a hiding place for a treasure chest? It wouldn't take long to find out.

He levered himself out of the cockpit and onto the ledge. With trembling hands he tied the kayak's rope to the iron ring. He could smell the damp rocks all around him.

The ledge was slippery – it must be under water at high tide. Andy took careful steps, back, back, until he could reach the rock wall. He shone his light along it to the cavity. Took three more steps and slipped inside.

There was no chest, and no treasure.

What there was, was a tunnel in the rock, barely big enough for him to stand upright.

Andy crouched low and crept into the tunnel.

◆◆◆◆◆

"ANDY-Y-Y!" Jen shouted his name till she was hoarse. It was an hour later and there was no answer. No sign of him, or her kayak.

"What has he gone and done?" Jen moaned to herself. "Why was I ever so dumb as to let him take the kayak in there alone?" They'd left the horses tied up on the other side of the island, without fresh water for almost two hours. They needed to get back, now.

Jen untied the skiff's rope and shoved it into the water. She hoisted the propeller and popped up the thole pins. Thank heaven they had oars, even if one was old and half-broken.

Rowing with all her strength, Jen sped towards the cave entrance. The sea was rising, the swells getting higher and closer together. Not only that – the tide was rising, too. She needed to find Andy and get him out of that cave.

Jen rowed into the wide entrance and then turned the skiff so she was rowing backward, stern first, and could see where she was going. She rested the oars while she found her light. It wasn't a powerful flashlight, just a small pocket one she always carried.

Its beam caught a streak of red in the depths of the cave. Her kayak!

"An-dy!" Jen screamed again. Why didn't he answer? Where was he? Jen didn't let herself think about the dark water on either side of the skiff. He couldn't be down in that black, bottomless water.

She rowed up to the kayak, trying not to panic. She saw the iron ring in the rock.

Where had he gone? The ledge where the kayak was tied was almost under water. Jen pulled the skiff alongside and jumped out. She tied the boat to the same ring as the Seahorse, and shone her light along the back of the ledge.

The cavity beckoned. Jen looked back at the boats, and the curved mouth of the cave like a down-turned grin. At high tide the whole entrance would be under water.

Jen took a deep, shuddering breath and climbed into the low tunnel. It was the only place Andy could be.

◆◆◆◆◆

Andy didn't hear Jen's shouts from outside the cave. He was stuck. Half an hour before he'd been climbing upwards, shining his light on the tunnel ahead.

In places, it had narrowed, and he had to duck and squirm to get through.

In other places, rotting cedar beams were pressed into the tunnel's sides in a kind of cribbing. Andy thought the whole tunnel might have been lined like this long ago, but most of the wood had rotted away.

The tunnel must lead somewhere. At any second, he had expected to come out into a room, a stash like the smuggler's stash he'd already explored on this island. And there he'd find a strong box, made of iron, and inside would be silver and gold coins, maybe rubies and emeralds and other precious stones.

Andy had kept going.

The tunnel had narrowed. He'd shone his light ahead. This couldn't be the end. He'd tried to wriggle forward, dirt falling on his head and in his nose and mouth. Okay. Too tight. He'd tried to wriggle back, only to find, to his horror, that he was stuck. Something heavy pressed against his spine. A rock?

Now Andy lay panting in the dirt tunnel. He'd switched off

his light. He should save it – might be there for a long time. It was totally dark. "Help!" he cried every few minutes, sure that no one would hear.

◆◆◆◆◆

Jen, at the entrance to the tunnel, heard one of Andy's muffled cries. She was shocked how far away he sounded. "Andy!" she shouted back. "Can you hear me? The tide is coming up. We've got to go."

She heard another cry but couldn't make out the words.

"We can come back – but right now we have to leave!" she screamed with all her strength.

The only answer was another faint cry.

He must be in trouble, Jen realized. He was trying to tell her, but she couldn't hear. Moving as quickly as she could, Jen hurried forward. She hated closed dark spaces. It was as though she could feel the weight of all the earth and rocks above pressing in on her.

The tunnel went up at an angle, getting narrower. A chunk of rotten wood, loosened by Andy, hit Jen in the face. "Ugh!" She spat. "Andy, can you hear me, where are you?"

"JEN!" She heard Andy's gasp of relief. "Careful. Don't get stuck. The tunnel gets smaller."

"I can see that…" Jen was now on her hands and knees, moving upward. A minute later she saw the sole of Andy's shoe, and his jeans, shoved up around one bare dirty leg. "I'm here," she puffed. "Can you turn around?"

"I can't turn around, or go back," Andy groaned. "I'm stuck and there's something pressing into my back."

# Chapter 14

# Out of Air

Jen felt panic rise in her throat. "Don't move. I'm going to feel and see if I can find what's holding you in."

"Be … careful," came Andy's faint voice. She knew he was embarrassed, but too scared to refuse to let her try to get him out of there.

Jen felt carefully up Andy's leg, around his hips and back. "It feels like wood." She was afraid any movement could bring the old beam down harder on Andy, squishing his spine. "I'm going to try to hold it, and you move, just a bit at a time and see if you can get out." Jen tried to keep her voice as calm as she could.

She got herself in position, lying beside Andy's legs, pushing up on the rotting wood. "Okay, when I say move, suck in your breath and try." Jen took a deep breath herself and cried "MOVE, NOW!"

Andy squirmed under her. "It's working."

Jen's arms ached like they were falling off. She couldn't budge the beam but she must be giving Andy the confidence to try to move. "Okay, again. MOVE!"

This time Andy backed out as far as his shoulders. The trickiest part was next, freeing his head. Jen pushed up on the beam with all her strength. "NOW!"

Andy gave a final wriggle under her and then they were face to face in the dark tunnel.

"Th-thanks," he mumbled, "Can you get off me?"

"Sorry." Jen scrambled backwards. "Are you all right?"

"I'm okay. Let's get out of here."

They scuttled backwards like crabs down the tunnel. When it got wide enough they turned around and hurried forward.

It was the water that stopped them.

The tunnel got damp, then muddy, then they were splashing through ankle-high water.

"Where did all this come from?" Andy gasped.

Jen dipped her finger in and tasted it. Salty. "This is sea water," she told Andy. "The tunnel is flooding with the tide."

"That means we couldn't escape even if we got to the boats," Andy said desperately. "The whole cave entrance must be under water."

"It's worse than that." Jen wiped her wet hand on her jeans. "If this whole tunnel floods there won't be any air." Her terror of closed spaces seemed to grip her by the throat.

◆◆◆◆◆

Kelsie stood with a bowl of green bean salad in her hands and her eyes on the door of the Dark Cove Community Hall. There was a potluck supper after the town meeting. Everybody brought something to eat or drink.

Where were Jen and Andy? Kelsie's hands, holding the bowl, felt clammy with nerves. She should never have let the two of them go off treasure hunting without her. It was getting late. Six-thirty.

Aunt Maggie hadn't noticed. She was too busy helping to organize the long table where the food was spread out. She might not even realize that Andy had taken the boat and gone to the island.

Anyway, Kelsie thought, Aunt Maggie wouldn't worry if he was with Jen. She thought Jen was sensible. She didn't know Jen had a crush on Andy, or that Andy was completely crazy about this treasure business. He could drag Jen into all kinds of trouble.

She looked around for Gabriel. Aunt Maggie said everybody in Dark Cove turned out for potluck dinners, but there was no sign of Gabe's dark curly head above the crowd at the food table.

Kelsie put her bowl of salad down on the table with a thump and flew out of the hall, down the steps and across the rocks to the Peters' dock. She was afraid Gabe wouldn't be glad to see her, but there was no one else to ask for help.

Whitecaps were forming far out in the cove and the *Suzanne* was dancing up and down at her mooring. They might be in for a stormy night.

The wind blew Kelsie's hair back from her face as she skidded up to the *Suzanne*. Gabe was there, washing down the deck with a bucket. He looked up at Kelsie in surprise. "I didn't think you were speaking to me," he said with a teasing smile. "Did your Aunt Maggie send you to tell me that dinner's ready? Tempt me with her bumbleberry pie?"

"Aunt Maggie didn't make bumbleberry pie this time," Kelsie gasped. "Bean salad."

"Too bad." Gabriel stopped teasing and hopped over the side of the *Suzanne* to stand beside her. "So I guess you ran all the way down here to tell me you're still mad about us turning down Speers' plan?"

Kelsie shook her head violently. "It's got nothing to do with Mr. Speers. I mean, yes, I am mad at you about that, but this is about Andy and Jen."

Gabriel put down the bucket in his hands. "What's the matter now?" He took her hand in his large strong one. "Are you annoyed that Andy's trying to take your friend away?"

"No. I mean that's not the problem," Kelsie tried to explain, distracted by the touch of his hand. "You know how Andy's got this idea about treasure on Saddle Island?"

Gabe raised his eyebrows. "I know he talks about it, but I didn't think he was serious."

"Dead serious," Kelsie gulped. She tried to explain, her words tumbling over each other, "Sailor found an arrow rock and then we saw this shallow pit in the middle of the island. Andy and Jen went off to dig there first thing this morning. They aren't back."

Gabe glanced at his watch. "And they should be?"

"Of course they should be." Kelsie loved the feeling of holding hands with Gabe, but why did he have to be so slow to understand? She pointed out at the whitecaps. "The wind's picking up. I'm worried that if they get back too late we'll never be allowed to go back to the island. You know how Aunt Maggie is."

Gabe nodded again. His dark eyes were serious now. "You think they might be in some kind of trouble?"

"They must be, or they'd be here," Kelsie said. "I'd go and look for them but they took both boats – Andy's skiff and Jen's kayak." She looked up at him, pleading. "Can you help?"

Gabriel didn't say anything. Letting go of her hand, he jumped back on the *Suzanne's* deck and disappeared in the wheelhouse. When he came back he was carrying two life vests.

"Put this on." He handed her one. "And come with me."

He led the way up the dock to the Peters' boathouse. Inside he switched on a light. A bright orange inflatable boat floated inside, with a forty horsepower motor fastened to the back. The name *Stormy Fool* was stenciled on her side.

"The *Suzanne* is too slow and I've been dying for an excuse to take this baby out for a trial run." He gestured Kelsie to climb down the ladder to the inflatable. "We just got her, and she's supposed to fly."

While Kelsie got settled in the boat, Gabriel opened the boathouse doors. "Hang on," he sang out as he jumped aboard. With a deafening roar, the engine sprang into life, and the light rubber boat zoomed out of the boathouse and headed for the string of islands.

Kelsie gripped the lifelines as they bounced over the waves. The speed drove everything out of her head, and in no time they were swinging into the landing place on Saddle Island.

To Kelsie's astonishment, Sailor and Zeke were tied up nearby, with their saddles and bridles in a heap on the ground.

"There's no sign of the skiff or the kayak," Gabe shouted, as he killed the motor.

"This doesn't make sense!" Kelsie cried. "Why would they leave the horses *here* if they were digging in the middle of the island?"

"They must have gone somewhere in the boats," Gabriel pointed out. "Any ideas?"

Kelsie shook her head. "I don't understand … even if they did … why take the kayak?"

Suddenly she knew. "Andy's been taking lessons in the kayak so he could explore an underwater cave down at the south end of the island," she said quickly. "We saw the place from the shore." She remembered the look of fierce concentration on Andy's face as he rode close to the cliff edge. Her brother was usually so cautious, so chicken, but something about this treasure hunt had turned him into a daredevil.

"It's on the ocean side," she told Gabriel. "Right down at the south end of the island."

"Dangerous place in this wind. Let's go." Gabriel started the motor.

"Just a minute. Wait." Kelsie sprang out of the boat and scrambled up the rocks to Zeke and Sailor. She stroked Zeke's cheek and brushed Sailor's forelock out of his eyes. "I wish I could take you back to the farm, but there's no time," she murmured. "We have to find Jen and Andy." Hurrying, she moved them to two other trees where there was fresh grazing and tied them loosely.

"Don't worry," she whispered into Zeke's fidgety ear, "I promise I'll be back soon."

Hoping with all her heart she could keep that promise, Kelsie jumped back into the inflatable. Gabriel backed the rubber boat out of the mooring with a loud rumble. They spun around and headed out of the passage.

# Chapter 15

# Loose Horses

Meanwhile, Caspar was unhappy at being left at the old island farm with Midnight. The big white horse prowled the fence that zigzagged from tree to tree around the pasture.

He wasn't afraid of the fence. He had a long memory and it included dashing through a wire just like this at Harefield Farms. He remembered the unpleasant shock, but it was short, and then he was through.

Caspar went over to Midnight. He whinnied and bobbed his head.

Midnight shook her long mane at him and went back to eating grass.

Caspar took a run at the fence and stopped short before he hit it. He could feel the buzz of electricity. On the other side of the fence was better grass, and somewhere out there were Sailor and Zeke.

Just then, faint and far off, he heard Zeke neigh.

Caspar kicked up his heels, raised his head high and dashed straight at the fence. The staples Andy had used to fasten it to the tree let go. The wire fell to the ground and Caspar was free.

Midnight raised her head. Like all horses, Midnight hated being alone. She trotted briskly to the broken fence, halted at the wire on the ground and then stepped daintily over it, flicking her tail.

The two horses headed for the shore, where Zeke was still neighing anxiously.

When they reached him, Zeke was already almost loose from tossing his head. Kelsie hadn't taken the time to tie him carefully.

Caspar trotted over to Sailor. He bent his big white head to meet Sailor's muzzle. "Don't worry," he seemed to say, "I'll get you out of here, bud."

He rubbed at the knot that tied him with his shoulder, nibbled at it with his teeth. All these tactics had worked to undo ropes before. Caspar was an escape artist.

In a few minutes he had loosened the knot so it fell away from the tree. Sailor was free, but his lead rope trailed on the ground.

Zeke's rope was even easier to untie.

The three horses and the little Newfoundland pony grazed for a while in peace. Then Caspar went down to the rocky shore and whinnied loudly. Where was Kelsie? Why had they been ignored all day?

Behind him, Sailor gave a short "Neigh." The pony trotted to the start of the trail across the island.

Caspar turned and trotted after Sailor down the trail. Midnight and Zeke followed him. Soon they were on their way to the other side of the island, heading for the south end.

◆◆◆◆◆

Gabe steered the inflatable through the wind and waves, up the eastern shore of Saddle Island.

"Where's the cave?" he shouted to Kelsie over the roar of the engine.

"Right there. Under that overhang of rock," yelled Kelsie.

"Are you sure? I can't see an opening."

"Go closer."

"I'll go as close as I dare." Gabe twisted the throttle to SLOW. The powerful engine died to a growl, but drove them forward towards the cliff with its bulging overhang of rock.

"It's right under there." Kelsie flattened herself in the rubber boat, trying to see any gap between the waves and the rock, but each time a wave hit the whole entrance was under water.

"They won't be able to breathe in there," gasped Kelsie. "The whole cave must be full of water."

"Maybe not. Some caves have a ceiling a lot higher than the entrance." Gabe's mouth was a grim line as he watched another wave bash against the cliff. "But if Andy and Jen are inside they won't be able to get out. By the time the tide ebbs, these waves could be as high as the cliff top. They'd never make it through the opening – they'd be smashed against the rocks if they tried."

Kelsie clutched the lifelines in terror, trying not to picture the image Gabe described. If only she was with them – if only she hadn't gone to that stupid meeting.

He powered up the motor to swing away from the dangerous rocks. "I'm going to call for help," he shouted, reaching in his vest pocket for a phone.

◆◆◆◆◆

As the wind howled around her blue house on the shore, Aunt Maggie slowly climbed the stairs to the two rooms under the eaves. She'd had a call from Gabriel, telling her he was going to find the coast guard diver.

She stood in Andy's doorway, looking at the rug on the floor with the green boat on the blue sea. Andy and Kelsie were out in the storm – and Jen Morissey too! Aunt Maggie's heart pounded and she struggled to catch her breath. It hurt to think of them in such danger.

◆◆◆◆◆

"I'm g-glad we're together," Jen whispered, shivering.

She and Andy had scrambled higher up the tunnel where it was narrow, but dry. Jen used her small light, saving Andy's.

"I'm not. I wish you'd never come." Andy put his arm around Jen's shoulders to stop her shivering. "This whole thing was a stupid idea, and now you're trapped with me, and we're going to drown, or suffocate in this tunnel." He hugged Jen closer. "You're the last person I'd want to hurt."

The warmth of Andy's body steadied Jen. "I know that," she said softly. "It's not your fault, and I'm still glad I'm here."

"Do you think I could kiss you?" Andy asked. "I've wanted

to, ever since I first met you. And … and I might never get another chance."

"Andy MacKay! What an awful thing to say!" Jen's laugh was half a sob. She leaned over and kissed Andy gently on the cheek, then on the lips. "That's all," she warned. "Seriously. We'll use up less oxygen if we stay calm and don't breathe too hard."

"Okay." Andy took a deep breath. It was hard to be this close to Jen without his heart racing.

They sat for a moment in silence, taking strength from each other. Then Andy said, "Jen – I think I feel a little draft. Not a breeze, exactly, but cool air on my face where you kissed me."

Jen traced his cheek with her finger. "Maybe my kiss was good luck. Maybe there's some air getting in the tunnel from higher up."

"Another opening?" Andy shifted excitedly. "Maybe it's a connection to the treasure shaft."

"Even if it is, we can't get through," Jen pointed out. "The tunnel's too narrow from here on. We'll have to wait until the tide goes out and the water in the cave goes down."

If Jen had known the weather that was blasting in from the east, she wouldn't have been so sure they'd get out, even then.

◆◆◆◆◆

"No service." Gabe snapped his cell phone shut and stuffed it back in his pocket. "We'll have to go for help. We need a diver."

"Leave me here." Kelsie begged. "Put me ashore in that small cove near the cave." She pointed to the notch in the rock wall where the trail to the treasure shaft began. Kelsie couldn't stand the thought of zooming off in Gabe's inflatable, leaving Andy and Jen entombed in the cave.

"I don't know," Gabriel looked doubtfully at the shore. "Leave you all by yourself …?"

"Please, Gabe. I don't want to be there when Aunt Maggie hears the news." Kelsie could picture her aunt's face. She'd lost her sister and brother-in-law on this island, in a storm just like the one that was coming.

"All right." Gabe made a quick decision. "I'll put you ashore if you promise not to do anything stupid, reckless, dangerous …"

"I promise." Kelsie nodded quickly. "Thanks, Gabe."

"I care about you kids." Gabe put his arm around her. "Things have been a lot more interesting in Dark Cove since you came. Andy's like a little brother and Jen's – family. Don't worry, we'll get them out."

But Kelsie saw the frown that crinkled the corners of his eyes as he headed for the shore. No laughing or teasing now. Suddenly, Kelsie saw Gabe as a man of the sea, used to disaster, storms and death. Her Aunt Maggie had the same expression sometimes when she looked at the ocean.

Kelsie gave herself a shake. She clutched the rubber sides of the *Stormy Fool* as they rocked close to the cove, then leaped ashore on a flat rock. The swoosh of an incoming wave instantly soaked her to her knees in cold salt water.

"Stay away from the surf," Gabe shouted over the wind and motor's roar as he backed away. "It can suck you right in."

"I know. I'll be careful." Kelsie nodded and waved.

Then Gabe was roaring away, going for help, and she was alone on the shore.

The wind seemed to take a deep breath, as if it was getting ready to blow its worst. It was calmer, suddenly, and the waves not so high. Kelsie heard a low whinny. She thought she was imagining things, but there it was again.

She looked up. Caspar, Midnight, Sailor and Zeke were working their way toward her down the rocky slope of the cove through a tangle of trees.

# Chapter 16
# Sea Horse

"Caspar!" Kelsie cried, scrambling up to meet him. "How did you …?" Caspar and Midnight had no halters, but Sailor and Zeke were still wearing theirs and trailing their lead ropes.

Quickly, Kelsie gathered the dragging ropes and tied them out of harm's way. "I'm so glad to see you, but how? Oh! I know, Caspar escaped and then freed the rest of you." She hugged his big head. "You're a bad, disobedient wonderful horse," she told him. "How did you know where to find me?"

She turned to Sailor. "That was probably your doing." She stroked his fuzzy forelock. "You remembered exactly where you'd been before, you smart little guy. You were likely on your way to the treasure pit, to find Andy."

She tied him and Zeke to nearby trees. Midnight stayed with them, but Caspar had already clattered over the stones down to the cove's rocky beach.

Kelsie waited. How long before Gabe got back?

The tide was going out. Damp green seaweed clung to the rocks nearest the water. Each time a wave roared in, it came a little less close to where she stood.

Kelsie climbed over the wet, slippery stones to peer around the corner of the rock overhang. There was now a small gap, a little crack, each time the waves sucked out. A bit more and she'd be able to see the cave entrance.

If only she had a boat. Kelsie could have cried in frustration. The wind was taking a breather now, but it could start blowing hard any moment. Gabe might not be back with help until it was too fierce for a diver to work. If only Andy and Jen had left the skiff or the kayak here in the cove.

Just then, Kelsie felt Caspar's powerful nose nudge her elbow. "Yes, I know you're here." Kelsie reached up to rub his cheek. She could feel his warm breath on her neck. "And I know you'd love to go swimming."

A daring thought came into her head. Caspar swimming into the cave with her on his back. They'd be lower in the water than any boat. They could swim in there and try to find Jen and Andy. Kelsie knew it was dangerous – for her and for Caspar. They could be dashed against the rocks, stuck in the cave.

"But it's better than just standing here," she said to Caspar. "I know you understand. There's the cave. We're here, and if anything happens to Andy and Jen, I – I want to be there, too. The three of us."

As soon as she said that, Kelsie knew it was true. "We'll wait a few minutes until the gap is wider," she told Caspar. "Then we'll go."

It was like waiting for jeans in the dryer. Just when she thought the tide had fallen to a safe level, another huge wave would crash against the rock cliff, throwing up a wall of spray. If she and Caspar had been caught by that they'd be dead! She shuddered, and waited – shoved a stick in the sand at the edge of the water and waited more long minutes until it was high and dry. The wind was still holding calm.

"All right. Let's go!" Kelsie stepped on a rock close to Caspar and from there to his back. "We're going swimming again, Caspar. You've got to be brave and swim into a dark hole – and not get sick again." Kelsie knew she was risking Caspar's life as well as her own.

*Sorry, Gabe, I know I promised,* she thought as she buried her hands in Caspar's white mane, getting a firm grip. Just going into the ocean was reckless, let alone trying to swim the big horse into the cave. She urged Caspar forward. He stepped carefully over the beach stones, then took a mighty leap into the surf, almost throwing Kelsie into the water.

The cold sea clutched her in its grip. "GO!" she screamed at Caspar, heading for the cave entrance. When the wave rolled back, there was room for them to swim inside, if they timed it right.

Caspar wasn't sure about swimming into a dark hole in the cliff face. He swam back and forth in front of the entrance.

"Come on, boy, you can do it. You're a brave, smart horse."

Kelsie encouraged him with her voice and let him know what she wanted with her hands and legs. Finally, just when she'd almost given up, he turned and caught the next wave, letting it roll them to within a heartbeat of the rock. Kelsie lay flat on his neck, the water splashing in her face. "NOW GO!" she told Caspar once more, and with a mighty surge of his powerful legs, he swam under the overhanging rock, into the dark cave.

"Good boy." She knew Caspar could see in the dark and her eyes were adjusting. She bumped against the skiff, floating free. No sign of the kayak. No sign of Jen, or Andy.

"An – dy!" she screamed. "Where are you?"

"Kelsie." Faint and muffled came an answering cry.

Kelsie felt her heart pound. She swam Caspar in circles, calling again. "I'm here. In the cave – with Caspar. Come quick."

Minutes later they appeared in the entrance to the tunnel at the back of the cave, their faces white and smudged with dirt in Jen's pale flashlight beam. They splashed through knee-deep water to the edge of the ledge.

"Hurry. We've got to get out." Kelsie swam Caspar to the skiff and caught the rope. She shoved and kicked it to Andy's waiting hand. "There's a high wind coming."

"The skiff must have come loose when the water rose in the cave," Jen gasped. "Where's my kayak?"

"I tied it to the ring in the rock," Andy gulped. "I never thought I'd be so long, or the water would get so high …"

"Worry about the kayak later," Kelsie urged. "Right now, start rowing. We've got to get out of here." She could hear the wind starting to howl outside the cave entrance.

"What about you?" Jen asked breathlessly. "Get in the boat."

"No. I'm swimming Caspar out like I swam him in." Kelsie gripped his mane. "We're going together."

"Be careful," Andy warned. "Horses have died in this cave." He pointed. "Over there, in the sand, I found a skull that looks like a horse's head."

◆◆◆◆◆

"Your Aunt Maggie's in an uproar," Gabe told them as they staggered up the Peters' dock many hours later. "You'd better get home as quick as you can."

Kelsie felt too exhausted to face her aunt. After they had managed to get to shore, they'd pulled the skiff as high up in the tiny cove as they could, out of reach of the storm blasting the island. The wind howled, and Kelsie, soaked to the skin, had huddled in Andy's jacket, close to Sailor's warm little body. He seemed impervious to wind, rain or the pounding surf.

The storm had weakened by the time Gabe got back with the diver from the coast guard. But they still faced the weary trek, back across the island to the old farm with the horses. Once they were safely tethered and Kelsie had wiped Caspar down as well as she could, Gabe had ferried Kelsie, Jen and Andy home in his orange inflatable.

Kelsie had wanted to stay with Caspar all night, but Gabe refused. "If you get pneumonia, your Aunt Maggie will have my ears," he told her. "I promised I wouldn't let you out of my sight again."

It was almost nine o'clock when Gabriel walked Kelsie and Andy to the door of Aunt Maggie's blue house. "Good luck, you two." He patted Kelsie's shoulder awkwardly. "I'll see you tomorrow, if your Aunt Maggie lets you outside."

"Thanks, Gabe," Kelsie said wearily. "See you tomorrow."

Aunt Maggie was waiting for them in the kitchen. For once, there was no plate of biscuits or homemade cookies, no tea or hot chocolate. Aunt Maggie's face was as gray as her hair.

"Sit down," she ordered.

Kelsie and Andy sat. Kelsie was so tired she wanted to put her head down on the table, wanted to change her still damp clothes, but instead she met her aunt's flinty eyes.

"This is the second time that I've feared for your lives on Saddle Island," she began. "Despite knowing how I feel about it, and despite my warnings, you've almost lost your foolish young selves to the sea – again."

Kelsie sucked in her breath. Here it comes, she thought.

Aunt Maggie swallowed and started again. "You two have frightened me nearly to death." She held her hand to her chest. "I don't know ... what I'm going to do."

Andy and Kelsie threw each other frightened glances. "Aunt Maggie, we're sorry!" Kelsie burst out.

"It was my fault," Andy jumped in. "All my fault. I should never have gone into the cave –"

"No, you shouldn't have. Did you not think every bit of Saddle Island has been searched for almost two hundred years by your Ridout ancestors for that treasure? Well, it has. And tomorrow, there'll be some new rules, or you'll never set foot on that island again while I'm living."

There was something about her face that scared Kelsie. The last time they'd been caught on Saddle Island in a storm, when Caspar had jumped in the ocean to save Mr. Harefield, Aunt Maggie had been angry, but not like this. She glanced at Andy. He was looking down at the table, his face red, his ears flaming. That was how he always looked when he felt strongly, Kelsie knew.

"Enough said for tonight," sighed Aunt Maggie, standing up and leaning on the table with her hands stretched out to support her weight. Kelsie could see the blue veins like cords on the backs of her hands, and her long, strong fingers.

"Aunt Maggie ..." Andy lifted his head.

"I'm too tired to talk any more," Aunt Maggie said. "Go to bed. In the morning, as I said, there'll be some new rules for you two."

# Chapter 17
# Wake Up Call

Kelsie woke up at dawn. She slunk downstairs and saw with surprise that her aunt's bedroom door was still closed. She must be sleeping in – unheard of. Kelsie grabbed an apple and headed outside.

The storm had blown itself out overnight and the sea in the cove sparkled in the sunlight. Whitecaps still tossed on the waves far out, a holdover from last night's wind. The flowers in Aunt Maggie's garden were bent and drenched by the rain.

Kelsie checked the buckets in the barn. Overflowing. She dumped them out on the grass and stood looking at the old building. If only Mr. Speers had kept his promise and fixed the roof. She'd have to talk to him – soon.

Her feet seemed to take her toward Gabriel's dock automatically. She found herself almost running toward the turquoise and white fishing boat, hoping Gabriel hadn't slept in.

He was in the wheelhouse, with a mug of coffee, checking charts.

He looked up when he heard her footsteps on the dock.

"She let you out." He grinned.

"She's still asleep. I didn't want to wake her up."

"You mean, you couldn't stand to stay inside on such a great day. Want some coffee to go with that apple?"

Kelsie looked down at the apple in her hand. "No. I don't drink coffee."

"Of course you don't – I keep forgetting how young you are." Gabe shook his head. "Listen, Kelsie MacKay, I was very mad at you last night for breaking your promise not to do anything dangerous."

"I know, but –"

"But if you hadn't, Jen and Andy might never have gotten out of that cave. You made the right choice. It was reckless, but it took courage. Sometimes, I have to admit, you act a lot older than thirteen."

Kelsie returned his grin. "Thank you, Gabriel. That's the first nice thing anybody's said to me in a while." She perched on a bench in the wheelhouse. "It was really Caspar that was courageous." She gulped. "Aunt Maggie was so upset last night she could hardly speak. What if she wants us to stop going to the island? What will happen to Caspar then?"

Gabe raised his eyebrows. "Things are really that bad?"

Kelsie nodded. "I think the whole thing about money is really getting to Aunt Maggie. She's – different somehow. That's why Andy's so nuts about finding treasure."

Gabriel came over and sat beside her. He spread out the chart. "I've been looking at this chart of Saddle Island," he said. "It shows the cave Andy found. And look what it's called – I never noticed before."

Kelsie peered closely at the tiny print. "Cocked Hat Cave," she read. "What's a cocked hat?"

"It's the kind of hat ships' captains wore a long time ago," Gabe said. He sketched the shape in the air. It was the shape of the cave entrance – high in the middle and narrow at both sides.

"Like a pirate's hat." Kelsie felt excited for a moment. Then she took the chart from Gabriel's hands and folded it carefully. "Don't tell Andy," she said. "I'm sure Aunt Maggie will never let us go back to that cave, and we don't need any more trouble."

Gabriel nodded. "No, you don't. If there's any way I can help, just ask."

"Thanks," Kelsie said. "I wish I knew what she's going to say to us."

◆ ◆ ◆ ◆ ◆

Andy found Jen waiting for him under the apple tree near Aunt Maggie's back door when he went outside to look for Kelsie. She looked so beautiful, with her silky brown hair smooth around her face and her blue eyes and upturned smile, that Andy stopped breathing for a second.

"What happened with your aunt?" she asked.

"Don't know," Andy mumbled. He half-wished he was back in the cave, close to Jen in the dark, dirty tunnel. She didn't seem to belong to him here in the sunlight after the storm. He cleared his throat. "Hmm, Aunt Maggie's not up yet. What did your mom say?"

"She was mad that I'd taken the kayak out in the ocean. I think she's glad it got lost."

Jen looked so desolate that Andy longed to put his arm around her again. "I'm sorry," he managed to say.

"I didn't tell her about getting caught in the cave," Jen confessed. "She was up at Harefield Farms till late, so she didn't hear all the fuss when Gabe called the coast guard. She's pretty busy with her new job."

"Well, I wish Aunt Maggie would take it so calmly," Andy said. "She acted so weird last night. I've never seen her like that."

◆◆◆◆◆

When Kelsie got back to the blue house, Andy was sitting alone at the kitchen table.

"Aunt Maggie's not up yet?" Kelsie asked.

Andy shook his head.

"I'll make her some tea." Kelsie hardly ever had a chance to cook in her aunt's house, but before they'd come to live here, she'd done all the cooking for Andy and her dad since her mother died. In no time she had a tray ready with toast and tea, and was tapping on the sunroom door.

"Aunt Maggie, are you awake?"

There was a murmur from inside.

Kelsie nudged the door open.

Sunshine flooded the old sunroom from windows along three sides. Aunt Maggie's vivid hooked rugs covered the floor, and one she was still hooking lay on the table.

Aunt Maggie lay in her white iron bed, on a flat pillow, with her gray hair fanned around her face. She looked up at Kelsie in surprise.

"I've overslept. Heavens – what time is it?" She sat up, smoothing her hair.

"Thought you might like some tea and toast," Kelsie said, not sure whether to set the tray down or not. She had never seen her Aunt Maggie without her silver hair clips holding her hair straight back from her forehead. She looked older.

"That was thoughtful." Aunt Maggie reached for the tray. "Just shut the door and give me a few minutes. Then I want to talk to you and Andy."

"We'll be in the kitchen." Kelsie nodded. She made sure her aunt had a firm grip on the tray before she turned and left, shutting the door behind her.

"How is she?" Andy asked.

"I don't know," Kelsie said honestly. "We gave her a horrible shock."

"All my fault," muttered Andy. "I lost Jen's kayak, and made Aunt Maggie mad – I wish I could have yesterday all over again."

They waited, silently, sitting at the white kitchen table. A few minutes later, Aunt Maggie appeared in her purple bathrobe, with a small book in her hand.

"I might as well get this over with," she sighed. "I was thinking about you two all night."

They waited.

"If those horses of Speers' weren't over on the island, I'd have them trucked away today," she began. "I was a foolish woman to let that man talk me into taking them there in the first place. We can't even afford gas so you two can go back and forth in the skiff." She gave a long sigh. " But it would cost even more to ship them back to the mainland, so they'll have to stay, for the time being. That is, unless Gabriel would be willing to transport them."

Kelsie shook her head. "Not in the *Suzanne*."

"I didn't think so." Aunt Maggie looked sternly from one to the other. "But there will be no more visits by boat or on horseback to the far side of the island. It's too dangerous. And when you go to look after the horses, you must be back here by supper."

Kelsie and Andy nodded.

Aunt Maggie handed Andy the book. "This belonged to your great-great-grandfather, Malcolm Ridout," she told him. "He was always after treasure on Saddle Island, and he kept a diary of all his failed attempts to find it. He and his friends dug shafts that were never properly filled in. They could collapse, cave in, and you'd be at the bottom with no way to get out. That happened at Oak Island, down in Mahone Bay, more than once. People were lost in old diggings."

"Lost? You mean killed?" Kelsie asked.

"Yes, killed. And no treasure found, either. You read this, Andy, and you'll see. It's just a dream and you'll find nothing when you wake up."

Andy reached for the battered old book. "Thank you, Aunt Maggie."

"There's something else," she said. "I tried to call your father last night but I couldn't reach him and he hasn't called back." Their aunt went on, "He must be traveling, looking for work –"

"If Dad finds a good job, he could send you money again," Kelsie broke in.

"Yes, maybe he could. We'll hope he calls soon." Aunt Maggie stood up. "In the meantime, I'm going back to bed. I'm tired."

Kelsie and Andy stared at her. They had never seen their energetic aunt lie down during the day, let alone stay in bed.

"Aunt Maggie, should you go to the doctor?" Kelsie asked.

"No. I just need to rest and have no more emergencies." Aunt Maggie shook her head. "You two stay out of trouble."

"We will," they promised together.

# Chapter 18
# Zeke Stumbles

"We've got to hurry." Kelsie fretted, as the three of them climbed aboard the skiff later that morning. "We left those poor horses tethered all night. I hope Caspar's all right after his swim."

"I'm going as fast as I can," Andy grumbled from the back of the boat as he pulled the starter cord on the motor. "As soon as we get there I'll fix the electric fence where Caspar broke through, so he won't head for the ocean again."

"But won't he just run through the fence whenever he wants, now?" asked Jen. "He knows it doesn't hurt him."

"I think he'll stay in the pasture as long as we're there," Kelsie shouted over the engine's roar. "It's when we leave at night that we'll have to tie him. Wish the barn was fixed. We could keep him in there overnight."

The sea was calm as the skiff zoomed toward the island. Kelsie let her hand trail in the bow wave, and thought about how different it had looked just hours before, with the waves lashing at the shore and the sky dark and angry. The ocean was stormy and wild, just like her. Maybe that was why she loved it. Aunt Maggie always said she was just like her grandmother, Elizabeth Ridout. She had loved it, too.

Once on the island, they ran up the trail to the pasture. The horses, tethered near the spring, whinnied to be set free. It didn't take Andy long to staple the wire back to the trees and check that the solar panels were still working. Soon the three horses and Sailor were frisking up and down the pasture, kicking up their heels.

"Caspar seems fine," Kelsie sighed with relief. But she knew the flu symptoms hadn't shown up for a couple of days after his first swim in the cold ocean. There was also the danger of him having a relapse from such a burst of exertion after a long rest. She'd keep an eye on him.

◆◆◆◆◆

Over the weekend and for the next few days, the three of them went back and forth to the island, obeying Aunt Maggie's strict rules. Andy read Malcolm Ridout's ancient diary from cover to cover while Jen and Kelsie worked with Caspar and Midnight, Zeke and Sailor.

Andy looked up at Kelsie one day as the three of them sat by the spring eating lunch. "There's a lot about horses in this notebook. They even used them for hunting treasure."

"Andy!" Kelsie warned. "You're not supposed to mention that word."

"I know, but it's all in here. A team of horses pulled beach stones up that road on a thing called a stone boat. And you know that wood you and I found in the tunnel?" He turned to Jen. "That could have been walls they built to keep the tunnel from caving in. The tunnel was made by the pirates, but my great-great-grandfather and his friends shored it up with cedar beams hauled by horses."

"It was a long time ago. The beams have crumbled," Jen reminded him. "That's how you got stuck."

"I know." Andy jumped to his feet. "I'm not talking about going back in the tunnel. I'm not that crazy. I just thought it was interesting about the horses, that's all."

"I don't believe you." Kelsie challenged him. "I don't think you've stopped thinking about that treasure for one second."

"So what if I haven't? It's all written in here." Andy smacked the notebook. "Aunt Maggie says there's nothing buried on Saddle Island, but our great-great-grandfather came this close!" He held his thumb and finger together. "Just because he didn't find it, doesn't mean it doesn't exist."

Jen sighed. "People win the lottery, too, but that doesn't mean you should spend all your money buying tickets."

Kelsie reached up to stroke Caspar's soft face – he had come over to see why she was sitting still for so long. "Speaking of money, do you two realize that school starts in just over a week from now?"

"Jen and I will be in the same class …" Andy muttered,

and then flushed. "What's school starting got to do with money?"

"We can't ask Aunt Maggie for cash for books or clothes." Kelsie gave Caspar another pat. "I sure wish we'd hear Dad has a new job."

Andy groaned. "I wish I could find that treasure!"

◆◆◆◆◆

That afternoon on her way back to Aunt Maggie's, Kelsie dropped in at the vet's office to pick up some liniment for Zeke's leg. The brown horse had been limping since he'd stepped in an animal hole.

"I should really take a look at him before I prescribe anything." Dr. Bricknell rubbed his face when Kelsie explained the problem.

"The thing is …" Kelsie hesitated. "Zeke's over on Saddle Island. We could take you there in my brother Andy's boat."

Dr. Bricknell rubbed his lined face even harder. "You could. But I have to warn you, my fee will be seventy-five dollars for a trip like that."

"Seventy-five?" Kelsie gripped her hands together behind her back to keep them from shaking. She knew that Aunt Maggie could never come up with that much money. "I'm sure Mr. Speers would be glad to help Zeke –" she began.

"Paul Speers?" The grooves in Dr. Bricknell's old face deepened as he frowned. "I don't think so. He hasn't paid his own bill for boarding his dogs." He looked more kindly at Kelsie. "Describe Zeke's injury a bit more. Can he walk at all?"

"Y-yes." Kelsie was still reeling from what Dr. Bricknell had just said. There must be some mistake. "Zeke kept running after he stumbled into the hole. He can walk, but he limps."

"Then he probably has a tendon injury," Dr. Bricknell said. "Massage the leg, ice it down if you can and keep Zeke quiet. See how he does. If there's no improvement come back and see me. We'll work something out."

The vet stood up and went to a refrigerator in his office.

"Here's a frozen cold pack for now." He offered it to Kelsie. "Should last till you get back to the island. I don't imagine you have any ice over there."

"Thanks." Kelsie nodded numbly. She left the vet's office with her thoughts flying. Speers owing money? Not paying his bill? What kind of millionaire didn't pay his vet bills?

"He must have forgotten," Kelsie said out loud as she ran back to the dock. She'd go and see Mr. Speers herself. Tomorrow. In the meantime, there was Zeke, and he needed ice for his leg.

# Chapter 19
# Truth Hurts

The next morning, Kelsie rode her bike up the hill. She didn't look at the bare ground where the Harefield Farms barn once sat. There was a FOR SALE sign stuck in the ground by the gate. What was that about?

She rode straight to the farmhouse and rang the bell.

Jen's mother opened the door. "Kelsie. I thought you'd be with Jen, on Saddle Island."

"We're going, but first I want to see Mr. Speers." Kelsie looked past Chrissy into the dark hall of the house. "I have some questions I want to ask him."

"He's not here, but come in." Chrissy led the way to the dining room, which had been converted to an office. "Maybe I can answer your questions."

"I don't think so. Where is he?" Kelsie looked around the almost bare room.

"I think he's gone back to Boston." Chrissy Morrisey looked embarrassed. "The truth is, I've hardly seen Paul since the town meeting. I don't really know where he is, or when he's coming back."

Kelsie stared at her. "But he has to come back."

"That's what everybody says." Chrissy gave a short laugh. "Paul Speers owes money to half the people in Dark Cove, and they all want to get paid."

Kelsie felt her head spin. "I thought he was rich."

"Me too," said Chrissy. "Maybe he stays rich by never spending his money. Anyway, he's put the farm up for sale again. I'm wondering if I can get my job at the Clam Shack back."

"He hasn't paid you?"

"Just a small advance." Chrissy shrugged.

"Do you … do you know if he ordered any hay for our horses for the winter, like he promised?" Kelsie felt she had to know the worst, right now.

"I don't think he did." Chrissy glanced through some papers on her desk. "I haven't seen a bill for hay. I'm sorry, Kelsie. I think Paul wanted to unload those poor horses the easiest way he could, and you and your Aunt Maggie were the solution to his problem."

"But how could he make promises he didn't mean?" Kelsie thought back to the way Paul Speers had stood in her Aunt Maggie's kitchen, saying he'd fix her barn, buy hay, restore the farm on the island. "He made it all seem so real," she murmured. "He was so excited about Saddle Island."

"It seems to be the way he operates." Chrissy gave a deep sigh. "Charm and lies."

"Lies," Kelsie choked. "Thanks … I have to go." She blundered out of the farmhouse, not wanting Jen's mother to see her cry.

She picked up her bike – wheeled it to the gate and turned to look back at where the barn had stood. She remembered the first time she'd come there, seeing Harefield picking on Zeke in the yard. Hank Harefield didn't seem so bad now, for all his bluster and bullying.

She remembered Caspar galloping out this gate, running down to the beach in Dark Cove to dash into the ocean. How could the whole thing be gone, so fast? What would happen to Caspar?

Behind her, a truck screeched to a stop on the road. "Kelsie? Anything wrong?"

Oh, no! It was Gabe. The last person on the planet Kelsie wanted to see right now. He'd been so right about Speers. She bent over her bike's front wheel, pretending to peer at the tire.

"Something wrong with your bike? I'm on my way to the gas station. Can I give you a ride?" Gabe called out his window.

"No, I'm fine," Kelsie mumbled.

Kelsie heard the truck door slam and footsteps crunch on the gravel. "That old clunker giving you trouble again?" Gabe asked. The second time he'd met her, Kelsie had been face down in a ditch after her brakes failed.

He took hold of the handlebars to have a look.

She wrenched the bike away from him.

"It's all right."

"But you're not." Gabe got a good look at her face. "You look like you could use a friend – a shoulder to cry on?"

"I'm not crying." Kelsie threw her head back and bit her lip. "B-but I just talked to Jen's mother. I found out – oh, Gabe! I was counting on Mr. Speers."

"Here." Gabe lifted the bike and plunked it in the back of his truck. "Hop in and come to the gas station with me. I'll get you something to drink and you can tell me what happened."

◆◆◆◆◆

The Dark Cove Gas Bar was also a secondhand store, where Andy had bought his motor for the skiff, and a snack bar. Gabe and Kelsie sat at one of the outdoor tables drinking ginger ale.

"Better?" Gabe asked.

Kelsie nodded. "Yeah." She blinked up at him. "Mr. Speers never meant to help us, did he? It was all lies."

Gabriel gave a wide-shouldered shrug. "Maybe he was going to help, but when we turned down his plan at the meeting he ran away like a spoiled kid, taking all his toys. In this case all his money. He left you with stuff he didn't need, like the school horses."

"How could he?" Kelsie asked, anger flaring. "Caspar and the other horses aren't junk that you bulldoze and toss in a dumpster. They're not –"

She was interrupted by the crunch of tires on the gas station's gravel. A blue car, driven by a blond girl, pulled up beside them.

"Hey, Gabe, how are you?" The girl waved from her open window.

Gabe got up, walked over to the blue car and leaned into the window. Kelsie could see the blond was wearing a tight turquoise tee. She was looking up at him, one hand on the steering wheel, the other playing with her hair. She had long, tanned fingers, polished nails and a gold ring. Kelsie clenched

110

her own hands, rough and grimed with dirt from working with the horses.

"Coming to my beach party Saturday?" The girl's smile was all for Gabriel. Kelsie remembered how Jen had said every girl around Dark Cove was in love with Gabe. He was a rich lobster fisherman, the town hunk.

"Sounds good," Gabe said.

"Great, I'll see you there. One o'clock – don't forget. Bye." The girl gave another flirty wave, accelerated and drove away.

Gabe came back and sat down. "A friend," he explained, "from school."

"I figured," grunted Kelsie. He hadn't bothered to introduce her to his *friend*, because she, Kelsie, was just a kid. Nobody important. "I'd better get back to Aunt Maggie's," she said. "Jen and Andy are waiting for me."

"Are you heading for Saddle Island?"

"Yup," Kelsie gulped. "Zeke's got a sore leg and we have to treat it. We left Caspar tied up all night, because there's no barn and he might run through the fence again. We have to exercise the horses, and I'm training Midnight in harness …" Kelsie's voice died. It was hopeless. Mr. Speers was a liar. The farm was for sale. Gabe had a girlfriend.

The truth hurt.

# Chapter 20

# Fog

At least Zeke seemed better when she, Jen and Andy got to the island later that morning. Light fog swirled around the shore as they docked the skiff, but the damp sea air was warm.

"A few days' rest, massage and cooling his leg with compresses should have him back to normal," Jen said, after feeling Zeke's leg for heat and tenderness. "I don't think we'll need Dr. Bricknell."

"Good thing," sighed Kelsie, thinking of the vet's bill.

"How will you get cold compresses?" Andy asked.

"I'll bring ice in a cooler and keep it in the spring." Jen pointed to the wishing spring.

"And we'll wish for something good to happen," sighed Kelsie, "like Paul Speers choking on one of his computer chips." She'd filled Jen and Andy in about her visit to Harefield Farms.

"I knew Mom was worried," Jen said anxiously, "but I didn't realize it was that bad."

Early that afternoon, as the tide rose, Kelsie heard the mournful honk of a boat horn coming in to Saddle Island.

"It's Gabe's boat," Andy cried, jumping on Sailor's back. "He's at the landing. I'll go see."

He had started riding Sailor bareback, hopping on the pony's back whenever he wanted to go somewhere on the island. It saved time, saddling and bridling. "Aren't you coming?" he called to Kelsie.

"No, it's okay. I saw Gabe this morning." Kelsie couldn't face him again.

"Well, I'm going." Andy trotted off on Sailor, his hands gripping his thick mane.

Jen was curious. "What happened between you and Gabe?" She ran a soft brush over Zeke's glossy brown hide, following the direction the hair grew, taking her time till he shone.

"Nothing." Kelsie was grooming Caspar. He had burrs in his mane and she struggled with a comb to get them out. "He came along after I talked to your mom at Harefield Farms, so he knows that I know what a creep Speers is." Kelsie gave a vicious twist to the currycomb. She wished she had Paul Speers' head under its sharp wires.

"Oh." Jen swooshed the brush over Zeke's flank. "Did he say 'I told you so?'"

"No. He was nice, considering he was right all along about Speers." Kelsie tugged viciously on Caspar's mane. "Sorry, guy," she apologized to the horse. "You're not a slimy, miserable, low-down rotten liar like Paul Speers."

She turned to Jen, comb in hand. "Does Gabe go out with a tanned blond girl who drives a blue car?"

Jen tipped her head to one side, considering. "That sounds like Steffi LeGrand," she said. "Where did you see her?"

"She drove up while Gabe and I were at the Gas Bar," Kelsie explained. "As soon as she rolled down her window it was like I didn't exist."

"She's always after Gabe, but like I told you, he doesn't have a real girlfriend – at least not that I know of." She stopped stroking Zeke and looked hard at Kelsie's unhappy face. "I know you have a crush on Gabe, but he's too old for you."

"You think I don't know that?" Kelsie worked furiously at the burrs in Caspar's mane so Jen couldn't see her expression. "But what about when I'm seventeen and he's twenty-one? I mean if Steffi or some other girl hasn't snapped Gabe up by then?"

Jen grinned. "Then I'd say you'd have a good chance."

"Maybe." Kelsie stretched out her arms and examined the scratches and broken fingernails and thought about Steffi's smooth lovely arms and hands. She gave a deep sigh. "If Andy and I are still here in Dark Cove four years from now. If we haven't moved to Uranium city or some mine in the Arctic."

"Please say that's not going to happen." Jen leaned into Zeke's side to get him to move.

"I don't know, Jen. I've got this weird knot in my stomach," Kelsie confessed. " I thought Paul Speers was going to make all this possible." She waved around the misty pasture. "Now I'm scared. I feel like the island and Dark Cove and everything I love is just going to disappear." She smoothed Caspar's mane. "What's going to happen to us, old boy? And *you*?"

"We need to stop thinking about it," Jen insisted. "Let's ride down to the landing and find out why handsome, hunky Gabriel Peters is paying us a visit in the fog. Maybe he has good news."

♦♦♦♦♦

"Your Aunt Maggie said to tell you your dad called," Gabe called through the fog as Kelsie and Jen approached the boat landing. "He'll call back tonight."

"That might be good news." Kelsie shared a glance with Jen. "Or it might not."

Andy was sitting on the *Suzanne's* low side, swinging his legs. "Look what Gabe brought us," he said, pointing behind him.

Kelsie cleared away the clouds of alarm in her brain to peer at the *Suzanne's* deck. Long square beams were stacked from her wheelhouse to her stern.

"What's this?" Kelsie slid off Caspar.

"Timbers, for your barn roof." Gabe grinned down at her. "Left over from the new deck at our house. I thought Midnight could haul them up to the farm."

"Th-thanks," Kelsie managed to mutter. What were she and Jen and Andy supposed to do with such huge pieces of wood?

"Then, we'll hook up a block and tackle and the mare can help us lift them into place," Gabe went on.

"*We?*" Kelsie raised an eyebrow. What was Gabe talking about?

"I have some spare time," said Gabe. "I could give you a hand." He grinned. "But I'm a lobsterman, not a carpenter, so the roof might be crooked."

"At least the horses will *have* a roof over their heads when it gets stormy," Jen said.

Kelsie couldn't swallow the lump in her throat. "What's the

114

use if there's no money to look after them and the horses have to go to the meat auction?"

"Come on, Kel." Andy swung off the back of the boat. "We don't know that's going to happen."

"And in the meantime, we can *do* something," Jen added. "Prove that we don't need Paul Speers."

"I've never seen you give up," Gabe said. "Where's the crazy kid who swims horses into underwater caves?" He gave Kelsie's curly head a pat.

Kelsie felt the lump in her throat dissolve. "You're right. I'll go harness Midnight."

Cantering Caspar along the trail to the farm, she thought, he still pats me on the head and calls me kid, but just you wait Gabriel Peters! You're going to think of me as something else one of these days. You already like me, but you don't even know it.

◆◆◆◆◆

Midnight was magnificent. The black mare pranced with eagerness while Kelsie got a beam hooked on, then put her whole strong sturdy self into the task of dragging it up the road.

They worked on the barn until the tide fell and it was time for Gabe to steer the *Suzanne* over the rocks in the passage and back to Dark Cove. By that time, the fog had settled around the island like cotton wool, and the foghorns were blasting their warning from every shoal and reef along the shore.

"Don't stay too long," Gabe warned, as he backed his boat out of the landing place. "This fog might get worse."

He was right. An hour later, as they dragged the last beam to the farm, the fog thickened around them. Kelsie quickly unharnessed Midnight and set her free in the pasture.

"Don't worry," she whispered in Caspar's ear as she tied him to the picket line by the spring. "You'll soon have a comfortable stall for the night instead of being tied. We wouldn't have to tie you now, if you'd promise not to break the fence again."

She knew Caspar couldn't change. It wasn't safe to let him

run free on the island. He'd once swum from Dark Cove to Saddle Island, hopping from island to island. He'd do it again if he had the chance.

"That's why we can't let you go to auction." Kelsie laid her head against his. "You're a special horse, with some special bad habits that someone else might not understand. You'd probably end up in a can of dog food." The idea was too horrible to think about.

A final check of the fence and they raced down the leafy trail to the landing and the green skiff. The tide was far out now, and Andy rowed while Jen watched for rocks.

It was hard to see in the fog.

"I think we're safe and clear,' she shouted back to Andy. "You can let the motor down."

But as Andy started it up, there was an awful CLUNK! The propeller had struck a rock. "The shear pin broke," Andy mourned as he brought up the dripping shaft. "The motor won't run without it."

"We'll have to row," Kelsie cried, reaching for the oars. "It's going to take hours."

"And we'd better stay close to the islands," added Jen. "We can still make out the shore in the fog."

"That will take even longer." Kelsie dug her oars into the water.

"Better than getting lost," Jen insisted as the skiff surged forward.

◆◆◆◆◆

The lights shone through the fog as Andy and Kelsie hurried up to Aunt Maggie's blue house.

"We're late for supper," Kelsie gasped.

"I know. But we came as fast as we could," Andy said, "Wasn't our fault the motor broke."

"I don't think Aunt Maggie's going to see it that way," groaned Kelsie.

Aunt Maggie was waiting for them at the kitchen table. She looked from one to the other with her long face unsmiling.

"You've missed a call from your father," she said. "I talked to him. I'll give you his news."

Kelsie wanted to sink down on a kitchen chair but she held herself tall and straight. If Aunt Maggie's face was anything to go by, it wasn't good news. She wanted to be standing up to hear it.

"Douglas ... your father ... has a new job," Aunt Maggie began, "in the tar sands at Fort McMurray."

"The tar sands," Andy broke out. "Dad's a hard rock miner, not an oil man."

"That's where the work is, so that's where he went, I suppose." Aunt Maggie sounded very tired. "The thing is, Douglas thinks it would be best if you come and live with him again as soon as he can find a place for all three of you. Right now he's staying in a boarding house but he hopes to rent a trailer."

"A trailer?" Kelsie couldn't keep the sting out of her voice. "We're going to live in a trailer?"

"Housing's tight in Fort McMurray." Aunt Maggie looked down at her hands. "Your father said he couldn't come to Dark Cove to get you. You'll have to fly to Edmonton and he'll meet you there."

Kelsie stared at her aunt. "Aunt Maggie, we're sorry. We left in time, but the motor hit a rock in the fog and we had to row all the way."

Aunt Maggie rubbed her hand across her forehead. "It's been decided," she said. "Your father misses you. Naturally he wants you with him, and I think …"

"Aunt Maggie, we don't want to go," Andy said desperately.

"I know." Aunt Maggie paused, and looked straight at Kelsie. "I think it's for the best."

She got up, holding onto the back of the chair. "Your supper's in the oven. I'm going to lie down."

Andy and Kelsie watched in disbelief as she walked slowly from the kitchen, down the small hall to her bedroom. They heard the door open and close, and then silence.

Andy glanced at Kelsie. "She's not even going to feed us. She's never been that mad."

"She's not just mad," murmured Kelsie. "It's worse than that. I think she's sick."

# Chapter 21

# In the Fish House

Aunt Maggie didn't appear again the next morning for breakfast. Kelsie scrambled eggs and made toast for herself and Andy.

Andy choked as he tried to swallow the toast. "Do you think she's really sick?" he asked.

"Yes, I do. I checked just now and she didn't even try to sit up. She looks awful," Kelsie whispered. "I wish she'd go to a doctor, but she's so stubborn."

After the breakfast dishes were washed, they ran to meet Jen at the dock. The fog had lifted and the sun shone on her shiny brown hair. But her round face creased with worry when she heard Aunt Maggie was sick and her blue eyes widened when she heard the news about their dad's new job and his decision to move them to Fort McMurray. "I'll hate it if you move away," Jen gasped. "Maybe he won't be able to find a place for you to live."

"Sooner or later, he will. Even if it's just a trailer." Kelsie stared down into the quiet water beside the dock. In the rising tide, golden green rockweed danced in shafts of light. The thought of being away from the ocean, away from Dark Cove and Aunt Maggie's house was too awful to think about.

Andy slumped down beside Jen. "What's happening with you?" he asked.

"Nothing good," Jen sighed. "Mom hasn't had any word from Paul Speers except a phone message saying her check is in the mail. She says if that check doesn't come soon we'll have to go on welfare."

"What about the Clam Shack?" asked Kelsie. "Can't she get her old job back?"

"It's already taken," sighed Jen. "There's six people for every job here in the Cove – you leave, somebody grabs it."

"I keep thinking of the horses." Kelsie paced the dock.

"Who's going to feed them once the summer's over? There's no welfare for horses." She stared down at the green skiff with its broken motor, bobbing at the end of a rope. "I wish we could get to the island to set Caspar free, but it's a long row."

"Gabriel said he'd come and help with the barn roof today," Jen said hopefully. "We could go over on the *Suzanne*, later."

"If I just had a shear pin I could fix the motor." Andy had been looking down at his boat, too. "Maybe there's one in the fish house." He headed up the dock toward it. "I'll look."

"Useless …" Kelsie called after him. "You're not going to find a shear pin in that old shack."

"Let him go. It's better than sitting here worrying and doing nothing," Jen told her. "Anyway, you never know what he'll find in the fish house. Your Aunt Maggie never throws anything away."

◆◆◆◆◆

Andy pushed open the creaking door of the shabby building. Once it had held eel traps and fishnets, floats and boats and every tool of the fishing trade. Now, it was mainly full of junk, like the old oar they'd found. Some of the shelves were broken. Many of the floorboards were loose.

Still Andy loved the smell of the place, old cedar and the sea, and a salty smell that was probably fish. He poked around the remaining shelves, looking in the boxes and cans of leftover bits and pieces for a shear pin as long as his thumb. That was all he needed to fix his motor. Even a nail bent at the end would do—if he could find one.

There were nuts and bolts and screws and pieces of wire and there, right at the bottom of an ancient tobacco can, Andy found what he was looking for. It would fit, he was sure. He held it up between his thumb and forefinger in delight and headed for the door at a run.

Too fast! He tripped on a loose floorboard, the shear pin flew out of his hand, arced through the air and fell to the floor.

"No!" Andy cursed, falling to his knees and searching the dusty floor with outspread hands. It had to be there. Or maybe it had fallen through a crack. He pried at a loose board – it refused to budge.

Andy stood up and looked wildly around. Somewhere, on those shelves, he'd seen an iron bar he could use to pry up the board. He scrabbled through the loose collection of objects. There it was, on the shelf above the tobacco can.

He stuck one end of the bar under the loose board and pushed down with all his strength. The board groaned. Dust flew into the air and hung in the sunbeams coming through the window.

Again! Andy thought. One more good pry and he'd get the thing loose. He stuck the bar in farther and leaned on it again.

This time the board flew up so fast it knocked Andy back on the seat of his jeans. He picked himself up and looked down at the hole he'd made in the floor.

At first he was disappointed. There was just a dark space under the floor, and the shear pin had completely disappeared. But then he saw that the board had been covering the lid of what looked like a tin box.

Andy grabbed the bar and pried furiously at the boards on either side. Soon he'd lifted four of them, and made a large hole in the fish house floor. Most of what was underneath was just the floor joists – beams running the other way. But in the center of the hole was this box, neatly fitted into a cavity that seemed to have been built specially for it.

There was a ring in the lid of the box, and Andy pulled at it. The box had been shut for a long time and didn't want to open. Andy stuck the iron bar in the ring and pried up again. This time, when the lid flew open he was braced and ready.

He got down on his hands and knees and looked inside.

It was just another notebook like the one Aunt Maggie had given him.

Andy felt a rush of disappointment. Another of Malcolm Ridout's diaries. But why had he hidden it in the fish house floor, if it was just another notebook?

Andy pulled it out of the box and opened it with shaking hands.

Inside, on the front page, carefully drawn, was a map. A map of what? He didn't have a chance to find out.

"Andy!" he heard Kelsie call from outside the door, "What are you doing in there? Did you find a shear pin?"

"Yes, but I dropped it." Andy quickly stuffed the notebook in his pocket. He pressed the lid back on the box and the loose boards back over the hole. He knew he should tell Kelsie and Jen what he'd found but he wanted time to look at it. To figure out what to do.

◆◆◆◆◆

"I don't have a shear pin for you, buddy," Gabe said. He was down in the skiff, examining the broken propeller an hour later. "But it's a standard size. I can run you up to the Gas Bar to get a new one."

The *Suzanne* was tied up to Aunt Maggie's dock, loaded with sheets of metal roofing.

"Can you get the shear pin later tonight?" Kelsie was dancing from one foot to the other. "I want to get to Saddle Island – let Caspar free, work on the barn roof."

Sure," Andy shrugged. "No problem."

Kelsie whirled and gaped at her brother. What was wrong with Andy? Normally he'd argue that his skiff came first and he had to fix it – why was he agreeing to go to the island in Gabe's boat so easily?

It's Aunt Maggie, Kelsie realized. He's really worried about her. That's why he isn't kicking up a fuss about getting his boat fixed. He doesn't want to make waves.

The sea slapped against the *Suzanne's* side as they made the passage. Gabriel had roped down the roofing sheets so they wouldn't blow off the deck, but they still clanged and banged together in the wind.

"Good thing we're not fishing," Gabe shouted at Kelsie over the noise. "We'd scare every fish from here to Halifax."

She grinned back at him. It was impossible to feel hopeless on Gabriel's boat, chugging toward Saddle Island with the sun glinting off the water, and the horses waiting.

She felt that way all morning, while Midnight pulled the rest of the beams to the barn, while they lugged and carried

122

and dragged the metal sheets to cover the beams and while Gabe sat astride the ridgepole of the barn, hooking up the block and tackle that would lift the roof into place. She was working too hard to worry about the future.

But when they took a break to eat their lunch around the spring, reality came crashing back. She and Andy were going to lose all this. It was no use fixing the old barn, because horses would never live in it. She and Andy were moving across the continent – where was Andy? She gazed around the sun-dappled clearing. There was Gabe, stretched on his back looking up at an osprey nest in a high tree, and Jen, dipping her cup in the spring, but where was her brother?

"Jen," she called, "have you seen Andy?"

Jen jumped up. "He was here a second ago …"

Gabe said drowsily, "Maybe he went back to the boat to get something."

"Or to get out of work," Kelsie scoffed.

Andy had done neither. He had been trying all morning to get away and study the map from the notebook under the fish house floor.

Taking advantage of the break in the work, he had jumped on Sailor's back and ridden to the bluff overlooking the passage between Saddle and Teapot Island. The island was clearly seen from this point, just a bald dome of rock with one small spruce on top like the handle to a teapot lid. The wind blew briskly from the northwest, churning the passage into a froth of whitecaps. As he tied Sailor to a stunted tree, Andy shuddered. This was the stretch of water Kelsie and Caspar swam across the night they'd busted Caspar out of Harefield's barn to hide him on Saddle Island.

It seemed so long ago. Now, Harefield's barn was torn down, and Caspar was living here, along with Midnight and Zeke and Sailor. Nobody was going to take his pony to a meat auction, Andy thought. The idea was disgusting. Now he understood why Jen and Kelsie had risked so much to save Caspar.

Andy turned his back to the wind so the fragile pages of the notebook wouldn't blow away. He started to read.

He looked up a few minutes later. Visions of trunks overflowing with old Spanish coins danced before his eyes. He'd been so close, that day in the tunnel. Just beyond where he'd gotten stuck, that's where it must be hidden.

Andy thrust the notebook back in his pocket and leaped on Sailor's back. "I don't dare even ask Kelsie and Jen to help," he told the pony. "Not while Aunt Maggie is sick."

# Chapter 22
# Aunt Maggie Leaves a Note

"A day or two and this roof will be done." Gabriel slid down from the eave where he'd been pounding nails into the metal covering. He stood back and looked at the low stone barn with its shiny new roofing. "It would have looked better with cedar shakes, like the original homestead," he said, "but that would have taken all summer."

"Thanks, Gabe." Kelsie wanted to hug him. "It's nice to know that some guys don't let you down, like Paul Speers."

Gabe's expression turned sour. "That jerk better not show his face around Dark Cove, if he knows what's good for him."

It was time to hurry back to the *Suzanne* and head for the Cove. Kelsie had already tied Caspar to his picket line. Midnight, Zeke and Sailor stayed near him by the spring, all four horses swishing their tails and munching grass.

Kelsie glanced back at them as they closed the gate in the fence. "Some night, I'd like to stay out here with the horses," she said. "They look so peaceful." She looked up at Gabe. "Don't you think that would be fun?"

"Sure," Gabe agreed. "Campfire on the rocks, hot dogs and marshmallows, sleeping under the stars with the sound of the surf in your ears. Mosquitoes. Rocks under your mattress. Maybe some rain. Sweet."

Kelsie laughed. He was teasing her again, but she didn't care. Spending a whole day with Gabe had been close to perfect.

As the four of them walked to the landing under the overhanging branches of old apple trees, Jen turned to Andy. "Where did you ride Sailor at lunch?"

"Oh, I took him over to the bluff facing Teapot Island … to see if there were any blueberries or cranberries," Andy said quickly.

Jen gave him a sharp look. "Were there?" she asked.

"Were there what?"

"Berries. Did you find any?" Jen knew by the way Andy's ears were turning red that there was something he wasn't telling her. He'd been quiet all day – ever since the fish house. There was something on his mind.

◆◆◆◆◆

Gabe dropped them off at Aunt Maggie's dock. "I'll come by after dinner and we'll go buy a shear pin for the skiff," he promised Andy.

"Okay." Andy shoved the *Suzanne* away from the dock and slung the bow rope aboard. "See you later."

"He looks like he's been around fishing boats all his life," Jen sighed. "Did you see how he tossed that rope to Gabe?"

Kelsie nodded. "*Suzanne* is his dreamboat and Gabe is his hero. He's trying to learn how to be just like him."

"Or maybe the Maritimes is in his blood," said Jen. "I mean everyone in your family's been a fisherman for generations."

"Everyone except Dad," muttered Kelsie. She took Jen's hand. "Can you come in with us?" she asked. "I don't want to face Aunt Maggie by myself."

"Sure, for a bit," Jen agreed. "I know what you mean. My mom's been as cross as a singed cat since Paul Speers took off. It's worrying about money that does it."

The two girls opened the back shed door and slipped inside. There was a strange silence in the house, and no smell of dinner cooking.

With a tight feeling in her chest, Kelsie stepped into the quiet kitchen. "Aunt Maggie?" she called.

No answer. But there was a note on the table, hastily scribbled on the back of an envelope.

*"Kelsie, I've taken myself to the emergency clinic. Feeling a bit off. Go to Jen's.*

*Love, Aunt M."*

There was a phone number scrawled under the message.

Kelsie handed the note to Jen.

"What is it?" Andy came into the kitchen. He looked from one shocked face to the other.

"Aunt Maggie's in the emergency clinic. She must have felt terrible to go ..." Kelsie gulped, thinking of her proud, independent aunt driving in pain to the local clinic. "How can we find out how she is? Is that the clinic's number on the bottom?"

"No." Jen shook her head. "It's the wrong area code. Come on." She started for the door. "My mom will know the latest."

Jen's mother was on the phone when they ran into the Morrisey's house. "Yes, I'll tell them. Don't worry about anything. They'll be fine here. Yes, I'll tell them to phone their father. Do you want to talk to them?"

There was a pause. Then Chrissy shook her head. "Of course. They'll understand. Don't worry, I will. Goodbye now."

She hung up and sighed. "That was your Aunt Maggie. She –"

"We know." Kelsie waved the note. "How is she?"

"They're doing some tests and keeping her overnight for observation," Chrissy Morrissey said.

"What does that mean?" Andy asked.

Chrissy straightened her shoulders. "It means she might need to go to Halifax for more tests and maybe an operation on her heart. The doctors are trying to find out exactly what's wrong. Meanwhile, she was anxious for you to call your father and let him know."

"Maybe she's anxious for us to leave," Andy muttered.

"That's not it." Kelsie took her brother's hand. "I know she loves having us live here, but she just doesn't know how she can look after us right now ..." her voice trailed off. She took the message out of her pocket. "I'd better call Dad." Her eyes blurred as she looked at the note. "This must be his new number on the bottom."

When there was no answer at the Fort McMurray number, she left a message. "Call us at Jen Morrisey's, Dad. Aunt Maggie's in the hospital. Here's Jen's number ..."

Andy was down at the dock after dinner, fixing his motor with Gabe, when the phone rang in Jen's bedroom.

"It's your father," Jen said, handing her the phone. They sat close together on the floor while Kelsie talked. When she'd finished she hung up the phone slowly, feeling the blood pounding in her ears.

"I think I'd better tell Andy and you together," she said, struggling to her feet. "It's about all of us."

Andy shouted as they came down the dock. "The propeller's all fixed – new shear pin."

The tide was out and the float was low in the water. The sun was setting behind them to the west. Kelsie thought of her father, so far away in Alberta. It was three hours earlier there.

"Dad phoned." She came slowly down the ramp to the float with Jen at her heels.

"What's the matter?" Gabe looked up. "Did you get bad news about Aunt Maggie?"

"N-no," Kelsie said. "It's not that. But Dad found us an apartment and he wants us to come right away. He says he'll buy the tickets as soon as Aunt Maggie, or someone else, can take us to the airport." She gulped and went on. "He knows Andy and I want to stay in Dark Cove but he thinks with Aunt Maggie sick the sooner we leave the better."

There was a long minute where no one said anything. A gull flew overhead, screaming. The waves lapped at the dock timbers.

"I can get you to the airport," Gabe said, finally. He scanned Kelsie's and Andy's faces. "But that's not the problem, is it?" He scrubbed Andy's bristly blond head with his fist. "You've got the barn, and the horses –"

"It's not just that!" Kelsie blazed. "We've got *Aunt Maggie*. She looked after Dad all those years, and Andy and me, and now, when she needs help, we're all taking off. We should be here, in the blue house, when she comes home from the hospital, and we should take care of her."

"I can see how you'd feel that way." Gabe smiled at her, and it wasn't a teasing smile. "If there's anything I can do to help –"

"Help us figure out a way to stay here!" Kelsie almost shouted.

◆◆◆◆◆

But Gabriel had no helpful suggestions and he soon left for home, putt-putting slowly away from the dock and waving from the wheelhouse. Kelsie felt her heart might break, waving back. "I guess we might as well get our pajamas and stuff to take to your place," she told Jen. It was just a few hours ago she'd been dreaming of sleeping on the island with the horses, and now she wouldn't even get to sleep in her own bed under the slanted ceiling in the blue house.

"Wait." Andy grabbed her arm. "Come up to the fish house with me for a minute."

"The fish house," Kelsie said, trying to shake him off. "What for?"

"I'll come," Jen murmured, with a glance at Kelsie. She knew something important had happened to Andy that day, and it was connected to the old shack at the top of the dock. She followed him up the steep ramp, along the dock to the fish house door.

It was dim inside, with just the light from the setting sun coming through the dusty west window. Andy knelt down and peeled back the loose boards.

"I found something – in here," he said. "In this box."

Jen got down on her knees to look. The tin box opened more easily this time. She peered inside.

At that moment, Kelsie threw open the creaking fish house door. "All right – I'm here. Fill me in. What's going on?"

"I found another notebook," Andy began. "I'm sure it tells us how to find the treasure."

"Not another treasure hunt!" Kelsie burst out. "How can you think about it at a time like this?"

"Hold it, you two," Jen said. "There's something else in this box." She stooped lower and felt in the corner where she'd seen a gleam of light reflecting off a small object. "Did you see this?" she asked Andy, sitting back on her heels and holding it up to the light.

"No. What is it? A gold coin?" Andy's voice was hoarse.

"I don't think it's money." Jen held it closer. "But I think it is gold, with some blue and white shiny stuff on it." She handed it to Kelsie. "Some kind of jewelry, maybe?"

Kelsie fingered the small object. "Not jewelry," she whispered. "At least not jewelry for people. This is a fancy bridle rosette. I've seen them on harnesses for draft horses, and they use them to dress up Arabians and Spanish American horses in shows and –"

"Spanish horses, like the explorers rode a long time ago?" Andy croaked, his voice high with excitement "Wow! Then this could be really old. It could be part of the treasure. It could be worth a lot of money."

The two girls gaped at him.

"The pirates attacked Spanish galleons carrying stuff from Cuba back to Spain and England," Andy rushed on. "The Spanish explorers had beautiful horses. If we could find more of these horse decorations –"

"Andy," Kelsie interrupted, "are you making this up?"

"No, it's all in here." Andy pulled the notebook out of his pocket. It was starting to come apart with all the handling. Flakes of paper were breaking off the yellowed edges. "This isn't one of our great-great-grandfather's diaries. It's a notebook one of Aunt Maggie's uncles, Uncle Walter wrote, before he went off to fight in World War Two."

He showed them the map. "I think we have to dig in the center of the island again."

Jen was still sitting back on her heels. "There's something you should know," she said. "There's a legend that the pirates put a curse on anyone who looks for their treasure. And your great uncle, Walter Ridout, never came back from the war. He died in Italy. Maybe he was … cursed."

Kelsie and Andy stared at her through the dim light.

"How do you know that?" Andy demanded.

Jen shrugged her slender shoulders. "I just do. Everybody knows everything about people's families in Dark Cove."

"Well I don't believe in curses." Andy stood up. He thrust

the notebook back in his pocket. "And I think Uncle Walter meant to come back and find the treasure, and if he couldn't … well, he left this map and instructions and the piece of gold bridle stuff for someone like us to find." He paused. " I'm going to look for that treasure … tomorrow."

# Chapter 23

# Last Chance

"We don't dare go treasure hunting again," Kelsie gasped. Her fingers traced the fine curled points of the rosette on its delicately engraved surface. It *did* look like something very old and valuable.

"Who's to stop us?" Andy said harshly. "Aunt Maggie's not here."

Kelsie shivered, thinking of Caspar's strange behavior at the shallow pit. "It's too risky, Andy."

"We've only got a few days," Andy pressed on. "It won't take Dad long to get tickets and arrange for someone to take us to the airport. If we don't start digging tomorrow, we won't get another chance."

"I don't see how –" Kelsie began. "Even if the weather is calm, and we can get back in the cave, you went up the tunnel as far as you could go and you didn't find anything."

"There's another way," Andy insisted. "We go back to the pit in the center of the island, the one where Jen and I cleared the stones. We dig straight down. According to the map in this book, the two tunnels connect."

"You've been thinking about this all day, haven't you?" asked Jen.

Andy nodded. "Even before Aunt Maggie went to the hospital I knew we should make one last try. It's like I dropped the shear pin and found the notebook for a reason. Now it's even more important. Like Kelsie said, it's all wrong for us to leave Aunt Maggie and Dark Cove."

Jen brushed back her brown hair. "Midnight could help," she told Kelsie. "We could use that block and tackle thing Gabe hooked up for the roof. Use it to lift the dirt out of the hole."

"Brilliant!" Andy cheered. "We could dig twice as fast."

"Wait a minute." Kelsie held up her hand. "Are you two

serious? Remember what Aunt Maggie said? That shaft could cave in."

Jen reached out and took the gold rosette from Kelsie's hand. "There's something real to look for now. I think Andy's right – it's worth one more try." She glanced sideways at Kelsie. "And maybe Gabe will help."

Kelsie rocked back on her heels. "Forget it. Gabe's too much of an adult. He'd try to stop us."

Andy took a deep breath. "Then you agree we should try?"

"If we do," Kelsie said slowly, "The first thing we have to do is make sure Gabe doesn't come to the island. We'll call him in the morning and tell him we're too worried about Aunt Maggie to work on the roof. We don't need the *Suzanne*. We're just going over in the skiff to look after the horses."

"Don't you think he'll be suspicious?" Jen asked.

"No," said Kelsie. "He'll be too busy looking forward to Steffi LeGrand's beach party. It's tomorrow afternoon. Saturday."

◆ ◆ ◆ ◆ ◆

Kelsie was glad she had the treasure hunt to focus on the next morning. It kept her from thinking about Aunt Maggie lying in a hospital bed. "She says she doesn't want *any* visitors," Kelsie sighed as she and Jen packed food for the island. "I'm sure she hates the thought of us seeing her so sick." She frowned. "I hope she doesn't need an operation."

"Don't worry. Your Aunt Maggie is almost as stubborn as you. She won't let a little thing like an operation keep her down," Jen said. She hoisted her pack on her back and picked up the bag of food. "But it's a good thing she doesn't know what we're planning today."

They had stayed up late, making plans for their dig. They had to make this one last chance work. Andy was already down at the dock, getting the skiff ready for the trip to the island.

If only the weather would cooperate. It was still misty this morning, and the forecast was for unsettled weather.

"That could mean anything." Andy had shrugged when he'd heard the news on the radio.

"On this part of the coast, it means expect the worst," Jen had muttered.

As they hurried down the dock, the mist was swirling around the skiff in gray threads. "We can't wait for this to lift," Andy declared. "We'll have to go slow and be careful."

◆◆◆◆◆

They left at low tide. Black rocks stuck out of the still water with even blacker cormorants perched on top drying their wings. The skiff crawled along the shores of Fox and Teapot Islands with the motor chugging at its lowest speed. When they reached the old causeway, Andy swung the motor out of the water and they rowed into the Saddle Island landing. They couldn't risk breaking another shear pin on those black teeth.

To Kelsie, everything seemed to eat up their precious time. Putting the harness into a large packsack, the traces got tangled. Caspar was twitchy, sensing the tension in the air, and Midnight seemed to catch it from him. Zeke, they decided to leave behind to rest his leg.

Only Sailor acted eager to go. "I don't need to saddle him," Andy said. "I'll ride him bareback." He jumped on the pony's back and galloped off.

"Don't get too far ahead," Kelsie shouted after the disappearing pony. "I'm bringing hauling harness for both Midnight and Sailor," she told Jen, trying to get the traces untangled. "Just in case."

She and Jen caught up with Andy on the trail along Saddle Island's east side. The ocean was blanked out by fog. In the distance, foghorns moaned in warning. Even deep in the trees near the center of the island, their mournful sound filled the air.

The shallow pit under the tall spruce was exactly as they had left it. Caspar refused to go close to the hole, pawing the ground and whinnying in protest.

"I know you don't like this place," Kelsie told him. "We'll try to hurry."

But Caspar refused to settle down. He butted Kelsie with his big head as if to let her know she was making a big mistake. Kelsie tied him firmly to a tree a short distance from the pit and turned her back on him.

"Let's hook the block and tackle to that tree branch up there," said Andy. The spruce looked very straight and smooth and the branch far from the ground, but Andy grabbed the tangle of ropes and pulleys from Kelsie's hands and jumped on Sailor. "Come on, boy, stand under that tree," he urged.

The pony tossed his shaggy head and trotted toward the trunk. "Okay. Stop." Andy carefully climbed to his feet on Sailor's broad back, took a few seconds to balance, and then threw a rope over the branch. In seconds, he had secured the hook to the block and tackle, settled carefully down on Sailor's back and jumped to the ground. "There. Ready to go."

"Amazing." Jen grinned. Andy might not be a rider, but he had won that pony's loyalty.

"Don't praise him – it will go to his head." Kelsie laughed nervously. She knew this whole treasure hunt was dangerous. She felt like Caspar, anxious, ready to run. It was as if the white horse could communicate his fears straight to her head. Something about the pit at the foot of the tree bothered him enormously.

They put a small tarpaulin in the center of the pit and, working from the outside, threw shovelfuls of dirt into the middle. When the tarp was loaded, Andy and Jen tied the corners together. Kelsie hooked it to Midnight's chain and the sturdy mare pulled the load of dirt away.

As they dug deeper, the pile of dirt grew and the pit narrowed. Soon only two of them, and then just one could dig at a time. In an hour they were up to their waists in the hole. By noon, up to their shoulders.

"We could never dig this deep without Midnight helping," Andy panted, as another load of dirt was hoisted over his head. While Midnight pulled the rope attached to the block and tackle, another rope lifted the folded tarp of dirt.

Kelsie was far down in the pit when her shovel hit something hard.

"It might be the lid of a chest!" She looked up with an excited but grimy face.

"Let me take a turn." Jen slid down beside her.

She boosted Kelsie out of the hole and started poking for the edge of the chest with the shovel. But everywhere she dug, the blade grated on metal. Jen got down on her hands and knees and brushed at the dirt. "It looks like steel," she called up. "Rusted steel."

"That doesn't sound like a pirate chest." Kelsie looked at Andy. He shook his head.

"Wait!" Jen shouted. "I found a ring, in the middle."

"Tie the rope to it and let's pull it up," Andy cried, thinking of the box in the fish house.

In seconds, Jen had the rope secured and Midnight hauled away.

Under her feet, Jen felt the metal tip. "Stop!" she yelled. "I'm standing on it." She moved to the other side of the pit. "Okay, try again."

This time, when Midnight pulled, the plate shifted, and Jen saw with horror there was nothing underneath it. "Help!" she screamed, clutching at the dirt, as her feet slipped into nothingness. "Stop! Back up."

Kelsie gripped Midnight's halter and pulled. The steel plate settled back, but on a steep angle.

Jen clutched at it. Andy, who had been watching frozen in terror, snapped awake and tossed Jen a rope. Gratefully she grabbed it and let Andy help her climb out of the hole. "Close one!" Andy grabbed Jen's hand and held on.

"What happened?" Kelsie ran to look.

"The steel plate is covering an open shaft," Jen panted. "I almost fell in. You're right, Kel. This is too weird."

Minutes later, Midnight hauled a metal square as big as a tabletop out of the pit. The three of them peered into a shaft that seemed to have no bottom.

"It's cribbed with beams like the tunnel from the cave," Andy said excitedly. "The two tunnels must connect. Make a rope sling for me, and lower me down so I can take a look." He reached for a flashlight from Kelsie's backpack and stuffed it into his pocket. "It'll be dark. I'll need this."

"Are we going to let him go down there?" Jen asked Kelsie. "What if the shaft caves in on him?" She was still shaking.

Kelsie was trying not to think of Aunt Maggie's warning about going down old treasure shafts. "Just take a quick look," she told Andy, "and then we're yanking you out of there." She tied a knot in a rope to make a sling and helped Andy secure the rope around his hips, while Jen tied the other end to the tree.

Andy lowered himself into the hole and then the shaft. When they could only see the top of his head, he looked up. "Goes down pretty far. Doesn't seem rotten. I'm going deeper."

Jen and Kelsie let Andy's rope out little by little, feeling the strain on their arms.

Jen glanced at Kelsie. "If anything happens to him …!"

Just then, the rope went limp. Andy had reached the bottom.

◆◆◆◆◆

Andy felt his feet touch the bottom of the shaft. He threw off the rope sling, fished for the light in his pocket and shone it around, On one side of the shaft was an opening, slanting downward.

The tunnel!

Andy fell to his knees and shone the light into it.

"Andy – what are you doing?" he heard Kelsie shout.

"There's a tunnel, it makes a turn – I can't see around the corner," he bellowed back.

"DON'T GO IN THERE!" Jen and Kelsie shouted together.

"Just a little way … just to see …" Andy muttered, as he crawled into the small opening. He held his flashlight between his teeth, wishing he had a miner's helmet like his dad's with a powerful headlamp. The thought of his father steadied him. Dad spent his life underground, crawling into small spaces. There was nothing to it.

Around the bend, the tunnel dipped at a steeper angle. Andy crept forward, trying to see. He could hear loose sand falling behind him, but he ignored it and went on.

Seconds later, he bumped into the metal box, loosening more sand.

It was lying on its side, almost filling the tunnel, open.

Andy squirmed around until he could shine his light inside. Empty. Scoured clean as if it had been washed with a power hose. Traces of sand were all that were left.

He'd taken this stupid risk for nothing. Everybody had been right all along – there wasn't any treasure. Choking with disappointment, Andy wriggled backwards. The flashlight fell from between his teeth. He scrabbled backwards, desperate, his mouth and nose and eyes filled with the falling sand.

With a muffled thump the whole tunnel collapsed behind him. Now the only way out was forward.

# Chapter 24
# Trapped

Kelsie and Jen heard a frantic whinny from Caspar as the tunnel caved in. There was nothing but silence from the hole at their feet.

"An-dy!" they both shouted.

There was no answer.

"I'm going down on the rope," Kelsie grabbed a shovel. "Stay here. Use Midnight to pull us up."

But as soon as she reached the bottom of the shaft, Kelsie saw it was hopeless to dig. Each shovelful brought another load of sand down to replace it.

She signaled Jen to pull her out. "We've got to get help," she said breathlessly. "Gabe will know what to do. Where's Steffi's party?"

"Whale Beach." Jen was staring, horrified, into the hole. "What – what happened down there?"

"There's no sign of Andy. He must have gone into the tunnel – the one that leads to the cave. The entrance has collapsed."

"He – he might be buried alive!" Jen's voice fell to a whisper. "It's the pirates' curse."

"Don't say that. Don't even think it!" Kelsie said fiercely. She threw herself on Caspar's back. "Andy can't get out this way, but maybe he can make it through to the cave."

Jen shook her head, remembering Andy stuck in the tunnel. "It's too narrow."

"We still have to hope. I'll meet you at the cove near the entrance," Kelsie cried. "Come on, Caspar." The big white horse was quivering all over, frantic to leave the clearing. He raced along the trail to the boat landing as if he knew Andy's life depended on it.

♦♦♦♦♦

Andy fought for breath. He could see the glow of his flashlight, still on, ahead of him. He wanted to cry but he thought again of his father, working every day underground, where every second there was the risk of cave-ins or explosions. If he started crying he was going to die down here. He had to keep his brain clear, and get out.

He struggled to reach the light, squirming on his belly. There! Andy grabbed the flashlight and clamped it hard between his teeth. He crawled forward on his elbows until he was past the chest and could get on his hands and knees. It would be a long crawl from the center of the island to the cave. And when he got there, the entrance might be covered with water. Just keep moving, he told himself. Don't think about the horse's skull in the sand, don't cry, just GO!

◆◆◆◆◆

"You're my hero," Kelsie whispered in Caspar's ear as she tied him at the landing. "I'll be back to get you as soon as I can."

Caspar nodded his head and whinnied as if to say, "Make it quick!"

Kelsie jumped aboard the skiff. The morning mist had burned off. The water was high over the rocks and she twisted the throttle to full speed. With only one person in the back, the skiff bucked and danced over the waves like a wild horse. They zoomed left instead of right, heading for the beach farther west along the shore.

Half an hour later, Kelsie waded ashore on Whale Beach, yanking the skiff up the sand. The tide was coming in. Above the high tide line, Steffi and her friends had built a monster bonfire. Sparks shot into the air.

Kelsie heard loud music and shouts of laughter. The kids at the party were drinking, dancing in the sand, throwing more wood on the fire.

Kelsie ran up to Steffi. "Where's Gabriel?" she gasped.

"Who are you?" the blond looked blearily into her face.

"Never mind. Where's Gabe?'

"Oooh," Steffi giggled. "He went over that way." She

waved vaguely toward the grass-covered sand. "Behind the dune, with some of the guys."

She was drunk, Kelsie realized with a jolt. Was Gabe drunk too? She stared at the sand dune at the top of the beach.

"I know who you are – you're that new kid who follows Gabriel around." Steffi was talking to her. "What do you want with him?"

There was that word "kid" again. "Nothing – never mind." Kelsie turned and ran for her boat. There wasn't time to explain, or to go searching for Gabriel behind some sand dune. She should never have come looking for him. She should have stayed with Jen. She had wasted so much time.

◆◆◆◆◆

While Kelsie sped back to Saddle Island in the skiff, Jen reached the cove. She jumped off Midnight's back and scrambled over the rocks to peer anxiously at the cave. The tide was rising. It wouldn't be long before the sea covered the entrance and her only chance to find Andy.

Jen hurried back to the horses. She put her arm around Sailor's fuzzy neck. The pony whinnied softly. "Your friend's in trouble," she said, choking. "Wish you or Midnight were good swimmers like Caspar – I could swim you into the cave. But you're not. We just have to wait for help."

Kelsie and Gabe should be there soon. Jen calculated the time it would take to drive from the beach in Gabe's truck, jump in his fast inflatable boat and race to the island. Any minute she should hear the roar of its big engine, coming around the south end of the island.

But the minutes crawled by. The wind picked up and the water rose. The fog had cleared, but the sky was low and threatening. Jen had seen skies like that. She knew a sudden squall could sweep in on them any second.

She prowled the shoreline of the cove helplessly. When would they get here?

To her surprise, it was Kelsie, alone in the skiff, who came slowly into view.

"Where's Gabe?" Jen cupped her hands and yelled.

Kelsie just shook her head. Close to the rocks she cut the motor, rowing in to shore. Jen clambered over the wet beach stones and caught the bow of the skiff.

"Couldn't you find the beach party?" she asked breathlessly.

"I found it, but they were all drinking. I – I didn't see Gabe. Never mind that." Kelsie shook back her hair. "Just tell me – is there any sign of Andy?"

"No. Wh-what are we going to do?" Jen stammered.

"I'll drive the skiff into the cave like we did before –"

"It's too late. We have to pull the skiff as high out of the water as we can." Jen grasped the bow of Andy's boat, tugging it up the rocks. "We're in for a blow. Look!"

Kelsie turned and gasped. A line of black clouds raced toward the shore, trailing a curtain of rain. The sky was inky and, below it, the waves frothed with white. They were almost fluorescent. She glanced back at the cave entrance, where large rollers smashed against the cliff. There was no way they could get in.

◆◆◆◆◆

When Andy reached the part of the tunnel where he'd been stuck before, he stopped. He recognized the beam, hanging at a weird angle across the tunnel. If he could just get through this narrow opening, he'd be close to the cave. He felt sick at the thought of being held in by the rotten wood, unable to go back or forward.

Now, Jen wouldn't be there to help him.

Andy shoved the flashlight ahead of him, through the opening. He sucked in his breath and very carefully, so as not to disturb the rotted cribbing, started through. This time, as soon as he felt part of his shoulders or hips feeling tight, he changed position before he was wedged tight.

"Think like a worm," he told himself. "Like a snake, slithering through the earth."

Before he knew it, he was through. Now he could pick up speed, scrambling for the tunnel entrance. Ahead of him he could hear a low, booming sound. What was that?

◆◆◆◆◆

The squall hit with terrifying force and the world became a whirlwind of spray, rain and pounding surf. Midnight took refuge in the trees. Sailor, built for gales like these, turned his back to it, clamped his tail and lowered his head.

As they yanked and pulled the skiff to safety, Kelsie and Jen heard the *Suzanne's* horn above the shrieking of the wind. They ran back to the water's edge. Gabe's boat was a blurred outline through the rain.

"What's he doing here with the *Suzanne*? He'll wreck her on the rocks," Jen screamed.

"I don't know – I didn't even talk to him," Kelsie gasped. "Take her out to sea!" she roared at Gabe. "Don't come any closer!"

They could see Gabriel in the wheelhouse, shaking his head. The *Suzanne* kept coming, till she was nearly opposite the small cove. At that moment a huge roller picked her up and tossed her onto a rock, as easily as a child throwing a toy.

"She'll be smashed to pieces by the waves." Jen dashed the water out of her eyes. The rain was coming down in solid sheets.

They saw Gabriel out on the rear deck now, trying to shove the big boat free with a pole. It was useless. The waves crashed over the shallow deck and Kelsie was afraid each one would sweep Gabe into the sea.

There was only one hope.

"Did you bring the rope and the harness?" Kelsie turned a streaming face to Jen.

"It's in the pack." Jen nodded. They clambered back over the rocks, harnessed Midnight and led her to the shore. The wind blew the mare's mane and forelock straight back, but her eyes were steady and calm.

"I'm going to throw you a rope," Kelsie shouted to Gabe over the roar of the wind.

He shook his head. "I'm not leaving my boat," he bellowed back.

"He doesn't understand." Jen pulled on Kelsie's sleeve. "He thinks you want him to abandon ship."

Kelsie pointed to the mare. "You don't have to leave the *Suzanne*. Midnight's going to pull you off the rock." She tried again. "CATCH THE ROPE!"

# Chapter 25
# Golden Spurs

Andy reached the cave end of the tunnel just as the squall drove water halfway up the entrance. Gasping, fighting the surging water, he half swam, half climbed out of the opening. The water on the ledge was waist deep.

The BOOM! he'd heard was seawater surging into the cave with each monster wave. So this was how the treasure had washed out of the box, Andy realized. Some humungous storm had driven water high up the tunnel, broken open the chest and sluiced the treasure away.

He was going to be the cave's next victim, the next set of white bones. Frantically, Andy climbed the ridge of sand above the ledge, struggling not to drop his flashlight or be swept into the rising water.

He was at the very top – there was nowhere else to go. Then Andy saw the water had sculpted a deep shelf near the cave's ceiling. If he could get there and squirm to the very back, he might be above the wash of the waves.

He could see the shelf, but he couldn't reach it. His wet clothes and shoes felt like lead weights. Each time a wave washed in he lost a little ground, slid a little farther down the sand. He made one final effort and grasped the cold wet edge of the shelf. Pulled himself, gasping onto it. Lay there, waiting for the next wave.

There was something solid and smooth at the back of the shelf, something wedged between the floor where he lay and the ceiling.

Andy rolled over slightly, ran his hand along its curved side in disbelief. Jen's kayak – the *Seahorse*. He clung to it like a life raft.

◆◆◆◆◆

Gabriel caught the rope on his third try, but not before a wave had knocked him off his feet.

"The next one will send him overboard," Kelsie screamed. "Let's go, Midnight!"

Gabe tied the rope to his boat's sturdy bow and waved that he was ready.

Kelsie stood behind Midnight, guided her as she threw her weight and strength into hauling the *Suzanne* off the rock.

It was no use. The water was more powerful, and the *Suzanne's* bow too firmly lodged on the rock.

"Try Sailor," shouted Jen. "I've got his harness, too."

In minutes, Sailor was harnessed beside Midnight and the two of them, the sturdy black mare and the strong little pony, were ready to pull.

Jen watched the waves, signaling Kelsie each time the water rose to give them their best chance of freeing the *Suzanne*. With the seventh wave, the highest, Kelsie suddenly felt the rope go slack and when she turned, she could see Jen waving, and hear the thud and roar of the Suzanne's diesels above the wind. She backed away from the rock, out into deeper water.

"Good work. Good Sailor, Good Midnight," Kelsie panted. She felt as exhausted as if she'd done the pulling. Jen came tottering up the rocks and threw her arms around her. They stood, holding each other for support. "Andy," Kelsie gasped, and Jen could feel her sobs through her rain gear. "He's still in the cave and the water's so high."

When they turned back to the sea, the *Suzanne* was disappearing around the southern point.

"She's on a slant." Kelsie pointed in alarm. "Is she going to sink?"

"I hope not," Jen said, wiping her eyes. "She must have some damage to her hull from running aground, but if Gabe can make it to the passage, he'll be sheltered there. He should be all right."

A streak of light lit the horizon, far out to sea. "The squall's blowing over," Jen murmured. "It'll go as fast as it came. Watch."

◆◆◆◆◆

Andy knew the storm was over. The booming stopped and each wall of water that poured into the cave was a little lower than the last. He clung, shaking, to Jen's kayak, watching the water go down. His flashlight slowly dimmed and faded out. The batteries must be dead. He waited in darkness and cold as the long minutes passed and the tide fell and the ocean calmed.

Finally, a sliver of light appeared at the cave's entrance. Then it was a thin crescent, then a quarter moon shape, then a blazing gap that hurt his eyes.

Was the sun out? Andy marveled. And was that the splashing of oars? It was – his skiff!

"An-dy!" he heard Kelsie shout with a catch in her voice. His bossy big sister sounded really worried about him.

"Up here!" he shouted back. "Jen – I've got your kayak."

A beam of light from a flashlight shone on him. "Are you all right?" He heard Kelsie's anxious question.

"I will be, when I get out of here."

"I-I've never been so glad to see you in my life," Kelsie gasped. The skiff rose on an incoming swell and nosed into the ridge of wet sand. She came scrambling up to him, reaching for his hand, her flashlight beam on his face.

Behind the light, Andy glimpsed the two girls' tired, happy faces. "Come on, let's get out of this cave," said Kelsie, shivering.

"Wait. Here's the *Seahorse* – careful." Andy lowered one end of Jen's kayak off the ledge to the waiting hands.

"You're alive," gasped Jen. "That's what matters – not my kayak."

"It matters to me." Andy gave a shaky laugh as he guided the rest of the kayak down to Jen. "The *Seahorse* is the only valuable thing I found in this dumb cave. She was wedged so tight up there on this shelf you couldn't see her."

"Let's go – this place gives me the creeps," said Jen, as Andy squirmed off the shelf and landed at her feet.

"We're going – and we're never coming back, right, Andy?" Kelsie was scanning the ridge of sand with her light.

"Right," Andy nodded. "There's the skull I told you about." He pointed to the gaping eye sockets lit by Kelsie's flashlight.

"You were right, it's a horse. Poor thing. I wonder how it got here?"

"Tossed off a Spanish ship by pirates? Who knows?" Andy glanced over at the skull, then stared. "Stop. Wait!"

"What's wrong?" Jen looked up from tying her kayak to the skiff with a long rope for towing.

"Something's different. There's more than a skull now. Shine the light over there."

"Andy – we have to go," urged Kelsie.

"No, just for a second."

The light zeroed in on scattered bones protruding from the sand. "Ugh!" Kelsie choked. "Some of those aren't horse bones. That looks like a human arm."

"Those monster waves must have uncovered the bones – I'm going to take a look," Andy whispered as he plunged closer through the wet sand. "More light."

The girls plunged after him.

"Look!" Andy pulled a long piece of forked gold with a gleaming spiked wheel on the end out of the sand and handed it to Kelsie. "What's this?"

"It's a spur!" Kelsie exclaimed. "But I've never seen anything like it." The spur had a gold buckle and was etched in tiny squares.

Jen shuddered. "Those sharp spikes would really hurt a horse."

Andy took the spur from Kelsie's hand and shone Jen's flashlight on it. "This could be hundreds of years old." He felt excitement like slivers of ice up and down his spine. "Let's put it in one of the kayak's watertight hatches – it might be really, truly, gold treasure."

But as they turned to the kayak they saw something that made them shrink with terror. The mouth of the cave was filled with water and in an instant it was on them – a huge rogue wave left over from the squall, sweeping into the cave.

Instinctively, they clutched the side of the skiff as the wave engulfed them. Andy gripped the gold spur with all his strength. They held on while it swept over their heads, then sucked back, threatening to take them with it. Soaked, flattened, gasping for breath, they lay on the sand as it roared out of the cave.

"Now … we're really getting out of here!" Kelsie sputtered. With all their strength they pulled the skiff back to the sand. "I hope the motor didn't get too wet to start," she groaned.

"We'll row …" Jen said.

"I wish I could find my good oar before we go," Andy started to say. "I know we'll never come back to this cave and I hate to lose it."

"NO!" Jen and Kelsie roared together. "We're leaving. Now."

Andy took one last look, shining his light around the cave. He grabbed Kelsie's arm. "Kelsie … Jen … look what that last wave did," he breathed.

They turned to where he pointed.

The whole ridge in front of them sparkled in the flashlight beam.

Andy's heart thumped violently. There it was – his treasure – spread out like a jeweler's display on a curve of white sand. "The water must have washed away sand that's been here for hundreds of years," he gasped, diving towards the glittering gold. "The next wave might take all this to the bottom of the ocean. We have to save what we can."

"You're right," Jen said breathlessly. "But let's hurry."

Scrambling, glancing back over their shoulders in case another wave threatened, Kelsie, Jen and Andy plucked ancient harness decorations out of the wall of wet white sand. Clean, shiny, some inset with precious stones: the gold objects looked brand new.

"Here's another bridle rosette," Kelsie cried.

"And another one." Jen held up the delicate gold ornament.

Andy found the other spur and a jeweled cross and a small dagger with a handle encrusted with gems. He shivered, thinking of the Spanish soldier who wore the cross and spurs and carried that dagger the day he died.

There were more bones, and in the flashlight's narrow beam, Andy imagined he saw the Spaniard and his horse struggling against the pounding waves just as he had. "That's enough." He shuddered. "Let's get out of here!"

They put the treasure they had found in the *Seahorse's* waterproof hatch and fastened it tightly. Kelsie rowed out of the widening cave entrance, with Andy in the bow and Jen in the stern, watching the kayak floating along behind them.

Outside, the sea was calm except for huge heaving swells, left over from the squall. The sky was lighter to the west and the seabirds had returned to their soaring over the cliff.

As the skiff grated on the shore, Kelsie heard a loud whinny.

"That's Caspar!" She leaped out of the boat and scrambled over the stones, expecting to see him run down the slope to the cove. "I left him on the other side of the island. He must have escaped again."

But when the white horse appeared at the top of the cove he was carrying a rider.

"Gabriel!" Kelsie couldn't believe her eyes. The sailor she'd last seen on the deck of his ship had turned into a rider on a white horse – tall in the saddle.

"You r-rode here?" she stammered. "You can ride?"

Gabriel threw back his head and laughed. "I moored the *Suzanne* on the other side of the island and there was Caspar, offering me transportation." He leaned forward and patted Caspar's snowy neck. "I think anybody could ride this horse. He knew exactly where to go – I bet he sensed you were in some kind of trouble."

"We were," Kelsie gulped, putting her arm around Andy. "But we're okay now." She smiled into her brother's eyes.

Gabe slipped from Caspar's saddle. "Good to see you, Buddy," he told Andy.

Kelsie wanted to hug them both, but she settled for Caspar, throwing her arms around her horse's powerful neck.

"I think you *must* have been drunk, to get on a horse," Jen laughed.

"Drunk? Who said I was drunk?" Gabe looked shocked.

"Steffi said all the guys at the beach party went behind a dune to drink," admitted Kelsie.

Gabriel frowned at her. "So *that's* why you didn't wait. I went behind a dune to get away from Steffi – she can be a –" He stopped, turning red.

"Never mind, I get it," said Kelsie.

"I heard your boat, but by the time I got back to the beach, you were gone. I figured you needed help so I drove back and got the *Suzanne*."

So that was the truth, Kelsie thought. She should never have suspected Gabe.

Gabe was still frowning at her. "I thought I'd come and save you," he said, "but you ended up saving me, and my boat."

A lock of Gabe's hair had fallen in his eyes. Kelsie wanted to reach up and straighten it, but she smoothed Caspar's mane instead. "It was really the horses that saved you," she said. "Is your boat all right?"

"A hole in her bow, but she can be repaired." Gabe's smile was back on his handsome face as he told them, "I should have brought the inflatable, but Dad took the *Stormy Fool* out with a bunch of scientists, and the weather didn't look too bad when I started –"

He paused and smiled sadly at Kelsie. "That's the thing about this coast," Gabe went on. "The weather's unpredictable. And that's why good boats go down, taking good men, and women, with them."

He's talking about my grandparents, Kelsie thought, feeling part of the history of this shore. It must have been a storm like this that sank their fishing boat.

Gabe went over and patted Midnight and Sailor. "You two were amazing. Saved my lobster boat." Sailor stuck his nose in Gabe's pocket, as though he expected a treat for his trouble. Midnight just tossed her head, as though she was above thanks. It was all in a day's work for her.

Gabe gave them both a final affectionate pat. "We should get these horses to the farm and then you three back to Dark Cove. There's news about your Aunt Maggie. She's in the

Halifax hospital having more tests. I can drive you down there in a day or so."

"Good." Andy glanced back at Jen's kayak, with its cargo of treasure floating at the end of a rope tied to the skiff's stern. "We have to find out about some things we found in the cave."

◆◆◆◆◆

Two days later, Kelsie, Jen, Andy and Gabe crowded into Aunt Maggie's small room at the clinic. They'd been told not to stay long, and not to overexcite Aunt Maggie, but this news wouldn't wait.

"Well," she looked up and smiled at them. "I suppose you've been keeping out of trouble while I've been a prisoner in this place?"

Gabe spoke for all of them. "We had a bit of a squall a couple of days ago, but everything on the island came through just fine."

Kelsie and Jen shared a small grin. The way Gabe put it wasn't exactly true, but it wasn't a lie, either.

"I'm glad you don't need an operation right away, Aunt Maggie," Kelsie said. "When can you come home?"

"The doc says I'll be clear to sail out of here by Wednesday." Aunt Maggie frowned slightly. "I had a small procedure called an angioplasty and if I eat well and take it easy I might never need an operation."

"That's good!" Kelsie beamed. "We'll make sure you don't work too hard."

"How long can you stay?" Aunt Maggie's asked anxiously. "Did you hear from your dad?"

"He'll be here tomorrow." Andy went close to the bed and held out a paper bag to his aunt. "But don't worry. We're not going anywhere. I brought you a present."

"Nice." Aunt Maggie reached in the bag. She pulled out the gold spur, and gaped in surprise. "What in the name of purple hollyhocks is this?"

"You know that treasure no one could find?" Andy said shyly. "Well, we found it."

152

"On the island," Kelsie explained. "Along with some other stuff. We took it down to the Maritime Museum yesterday."

"They say it's an important historical artifact," Andy said the words carefully, then grinned and rushed on, "Pure gold. Worth an awful lot of money. They said I could bring this to show you, but the rest is at the museum. They were really interested in Uncle Walter's notebook, too."

"Uncle Walter," Aunt Maggie sighed. "He was a real Ridout, an adventurer. He died in the war before I was born, but I know he was one of my father's favorites."

"There'll be enough money to pay the bills for a while, at least, and buy some hay and get the barn fixed," Kelsie said eagerly.

Andy broke in. "And we won't have to move away."

"Well," Aunt Maggie lay back on her pillow and smiled again. This time she looked really happy. The lines smoothed out of her forehead. "That's a wonderful present, that is," she said. "Lying here I've had time to think how much I was going to miss you two." She raised her eyebrows at Andy. "How are the new oars working?"

Andy gulped and blushed. "I'm getting pretty good at rowing."

Just then, the nurse bustled in and asked them all to leave.

"That was a lot of exciting news," Kelsie muttered as her aunt's door swung shut. "Hope we didn't make Aunt Maggie worse."

"It's a good thing you didn't tell her about Paul Speers," Jen whispered to Andy. "That would have gotten her blood pressure up, for sure."

"What about Speers?" Gabe scowled down at her.

"Maybe he heard about the treasure," laughed Andy, "because he showed up yesterday, with a crew to fix Aunt Maggie's leaky old barn."

"And he paid my mom," sighed Jen, "and took the FOR SALE sign down at Harefield Farms. He's looking for a new scheme, she says."

"I don't care what he does." Kelsie grinned at Gabe. "As long as he stays far away from Saddle Island. That's just for us, and the horses. Forever!"

◆◆◆◆◆

The day before school started in Dark Cove, Kelsie, Jen and Andy biked up the road out of Dark Cove to the boat builder's workshop.

"Stop here for a sec," Kelsie said, hopping off her bike at the highest point in the road.

The three of them wheeled their bikes to the edge of the cliff and looked down.

From here, the islands in Dark Cove looked like green jewels floating on a blue velvet sea. Saddle Island seemed farther away from this angle, and you could clearly see its saddle shape and the lighter green of the meadow near the north end. Kelsie pictured Caspar and the other horses grazing peacefully – the first thing they'd done with their money was rebuild a sturdy fence so he could be free. Kelsie drew in a long happy breath of fresh sea air. Her lovely, brave, swim-crazy Caspar was fit and sound and ready for new adventures.

They got back on their bikes and rode the rest of the way to Steve Murphy's boat shop. From the doorway they saw an old man smoothing the hull of a new dory with a large plane. Other boats, old and new, were stored along the walls.

Steve Murphy looked up and saw them. "I guess you've come to collect your oar." He nodded to Andy, put down his plane and straightened up with an effort. "It's over here – just like the one I hear you misplaced."

He handed Andy a smooth golden-varnished oar from a rack.

"Exactly the same," Andy said. "Don't tell Aunt Maggie I lost it."

The old man winked at him. "I won't. We know how to keep secrets around this place."